Fair Deal

by

Kamal M Malak

Kamal M Malak
13 Fernhurst Gardens,
Edgware,
Middlesex HA8 7PQ
UK
© April 2016

Copyrights © April 2016 by Kamal M Malak

No part of this book can be published, reproduced, copied or electronically distributed, lent in any format, without publisher's prior consent in writing.

ISBN: 978-0-9954528-0-0

First Printing – Printed in the United Kingdom

Kamal M Malak
13 Fernhurst Gardens,
Edgware, Middlesex HA8 7PQ
UK

Preface

My earlier novels 'Mr & Mrs Boheim' and 'A Friendly Deception' were criticised by some of my friends as being too descriptive of sex. In order to defend myself, I explained to them that it was necessary for the relevant stories, particularly, 'A Friendly Deception' where the leading characters were trying to have a baby.

Anyway, the current novel relates to the story of some solicitors, and Heavens forbid who has ever heard of solicitors being interested in sex!? They are so preoccupied with divorces, rape and adultery cases. But the story does start from a Christmas party in an office, and the excesses committed by one solicitor with somewhat drunk wife of his boss, in a lonely filing room. Another colleague, who had his eyes on the wife, sees them in the filing room by accident, and out of jealousy, makes them know that he has seen them in their intimate activity. This causes all kinds of repercussions.

So please forgive me if I have tried to hide a lot of description in rather dull words like 'in between the thighs', backside, and taste of Cadbury….. But then let me not spoil the story by giving away too much………

Chapter 1

A luxurious office block in the city of London. It is mid-December, and in the evening the area is rather quiet. Most office workers have gone home after finishing their work. However, from the outside one can see some of the offices inside, Xmas tree decoration and occasionally a string of Christmas cards. On the tenth floor, in the offices of Henry Sheldon LLP solicitors, a party is in full swing. Instead of having the party in a restaurant or in a hotel, they are having their Christmas party in the office.

Sir Henry Sheldon, an impressive man in his fifties, wearing a dark suit and a smart tie, is standing at the corner of the main board room which has been cleared to have the party, talking to a small group of solicitors and some of their wives.

'I do not think letting other profession doing the probate work has really affected us,' Sir Henry said. 'On the contrary, the clients still consider the lawyers to do a better service', he added. They all listened with interest, with one or two faces showing that they did not quite agree with his comment, but did not want to contradict him. Sir Henry took a sip from his Champagne glass and wanted to say something; then suddenly there was a little noise and the office administrator, who was in charge of the party, made some noise with a spoon on his glass.
'Ladies and gentlemen, the dinner is being served. Please make your way to the dining room.'

Next to the Board room, there was the office of Sir Henry's assistant, and a small library partitioned. For the party, it has been changed into a large dining room with the main board room table for about twenty people, and surrounding small tables and chairs. Everyone moves, the partners and their wives sit on the main board room big table, and other solicitors and supporting staff, with their respective wives, girlfriends and supporting staff sit in the close by tables. The catering staffs, in their smart white uniforms, serve the food and drinks.

About an hour later, the food is nearly finished, Sir Henry stands up; there was another spoon and glass ritual and suddenly there was silence. 'Ladies and Gentlemen, the senior partner Sir Henry Sheldon' Gordon Moore, the office administrator announced; everyone becomes quiet.

'My fellow partners, colleagues, ladies and gentlemen, I am sorry to interrupt your dinner but I will not bore you with details. Our LLP has had one of its finest years and made huge profit, the gross fees has increased by sixty percent compared to the last year and the net fees is increased significantly. It is our team efforts which have achieved it, and I am really grateful to you for all the hard work you put in. The practice also had a very good coverage in the press, and I am glad to inform you that his morning, I was informed by the Financial Conduct Authority that they have hired our practice for a major investigation into one of the hedge funds.' He stops for a few seconds, takes a sip from his glass and continues, 'you will see the promotion list in the New Year but I am very excited to say that Peter Cooper is to be admitted to the partnership next year. Peter, could you please stand up'. In the nearby table, a man in his mid-thirties stands up. Everybody claps. 'Thank you.' Peter said in a low voice and sits down.
'Well, I said I won't take much of your time, so in the end, I would like to say that the future is looking good; I am sure there will be many lawsuits in the coming year and apart from commercial cases, the public will continue to divorce and we shall assist them and reduce their burden including their bank balances with our huge fees.' Everyone starts laughing. Sir Henry stops for a few seconds and continues, 'on a more

serious note, I would like to thank you once again and wish you all Merry
Christmas and a very Happy New Year.'

They all clap while Sir Henry sits down.

It is about 11PM, the tables have been cleared and most people are
standing. In the adjoining board room with the doors open, there is
dim light and music is on. A number of people are dancing. Slow rhythm
music, Christmas spirit and a lot of fine wine and Champagne, the girls
are dancing very close with their partners. Everyone seems happy and
cheerful.

Chris Sneale, a solicitor in his early thirties, is going to the ninth floor
which was also occupied by the LLP. There were other solicitors' offices
including juniors, trainee solicitors, filing room and reception. He wanted
to pick up his coat from the cloak room. His wife Meina did not come
with him to the party as she was not very well, having caught flu. The
firm had arranged a cab company to bring all the attendees back to their
homes at the LLP's cost. They did not want them to worry about trains or
driving after the party. Chris was about to enter the cloak room when he
noticed the door of the filing room not locked. It was generally closed
and locked after the office hours, the cloak room and the filing room were
in the secluded part of the floor. Out of curiosity, he opened it slightly,
what he saw shocked him. There was no light but the light from outside
through the windows made the room visible. He heard some noises. He
thought someone was sick and crying in pain. He entered the room
further, behind the large filing cabinets, there was a sofa; he saw a man
on top of a woman, engaged in full blown intercourse. Chris stepped
back; the couple were far too busy to notice him. He moved behind
another filing cabinet carefully from where they could not see him. He
stood there watching them.

After a few more moaning, the man moved and sat down while the
woman put her legs on his lap; the sofa was not big enough for both of
them to lie together. In semi-darkness, he recognised them. It was one of

his colleagues, Lenny Crowe another solicitor in the practice. He could not see the face of the woman, and he was about to go but suddenly, Lenny stood up, he was half dressed, he pulled his pants; Chris noticed the face of the woman, it was Sharon Hamilton, the wife of his boss. Sharon pulled Lenny towards him. 'I am not finished with you my tiger,' she said in a husky voice and put his pants down. She seemed to be half drunk, she looked beautiful as ever, even more so now naked, her body so smooth. Chris was amazed, in spite of his mind telling him to move, he stared quietly, watching Sharon do an act on Lenny. He was aroused, she did it very well. He continued watching an expert woman showing her expertise on his colleague. He felt a sense of jealousy, so this is the upper stiff woman who will not even pay any attention to him when he met at the office parties or at their home.

After a few minutes, Chris decided that this snooty woman needs to be taught a lesson, he moved a little further. 'Doesn't she do well Lenny...Merry Christmas!' He stepped back and got out of the room. Sharon had a shock, they both froze. Lenny immediately moved and put his pants up; Sharon sat down and took a handkerchief to clean her mouth and face which has perspired. She was half dressed; she immediately did her bra and pulled her dress. She also slipped her pants quickly.
'It was Chris, wasn't he?' asked Sharon, not sure if she recognised the man.
'No, I am not sure, I did not see him,' replied Lenny, his face not so lit up now, and showing signs of worries.
'Oh, don't worry, he knows it is Christmas and everybody is having fun,' she tried to console him.
'I think we better get out of here and join the party before anyone else walks in here.'
'You said that hardly anyone comes here during the working hours, how come this idiot....' Before Sharon could finish her sentence, Lenny interrupted. 'Let's think about that some other time and get out of here.'

In a few minutes, they both were back on the upper floor, arriving separately where the party was in full swing. Lots of people were dancing and in the adjoining room, some were standing and talking. Sharon looked around, Lenny was talking to a small group; her eyes searched Terry, her husband, and she noticed he was dancing with Pamela, Sir Henry Sheldon's wife. Sharon smiled, thinking, this man will never give up his ambition. Why should he dance with an old woman while there were so many beautiful women around?

'May I, mam?' she heard a man whom she did not recognise.

'With pleasure,' she took his extended hand and moved to the dance floor. While dancing she asked,' are you American? Have we met?'

'No mam, I am just visiting London from Brookes Springfield.'

'The US Associates, right?'

'Yes mam.'

They continued to dance; Terry noticed them and smiled at Sharon. She smiled back.

'Do you know Mr Hamilton?' asked the American.

'Yes, he happens to be my husband… Mr?' Sharon said, looking for his name.

'I am sorry, I am Chuck Orcel. I did not know Terry had such a beautiful wife.'

'Thank you Chuck, you Americans have a knack of seducing women!' She said in a rather sexy voice. It seemed that the earlier shock in the filing room had not completely removed the effects of alcohol.

'I will try my best,' he pulled her towards him.

In a few minutes, Lenny looked at Sharon and Chuck dancing and was pleased that she was keeping her distance from him.

The party continued and Henry Sheldon LLP's staff continued to enjoy their Christmas till late without any worries of the next working day. Only, Lenny was worried.

Chris arrived home and went to the lounge. It was not very late; he was not sure if Meina was awake but decided to stay in the lounge.

'Is that you, Chris?' he heard the voice of Meina from the bedroom.

'I will be there in a sec,' he replied. He took his coat off and hanged it in the hall, went to the kitchen and poured a glass of white wine. He came into the lounge and took his jacket off and sat down. He took a sip of cold wine and felt better. His mind was working, the feeling of the party, his lack of 'success' in the party, and the last few minutes in the filing room, wondering why Meina never behaves like that with him. Suddenly, he started planning, how can I profit from this knowledge? Maybe he can blackmail her to influence her husband to give him promotion. Maybe he can threaten her that she should be 'nice' with him, at least a few times, so that he can feel the same pleasure as he saw on Lenny's face. Or maybe he should just do nothing and act as though he never went to the filing room, and behave normally with Lenny.

Chris was nearly half an hour in the lounge; he noticed Meina was standing at the lounge door in her dressing gown. Meina was a good looking girl. She had a nice light brown complexion, was in her late twenties. She was medium built and medium height. She was of Indian origin, though born in London and brought up in a middle class family. She worked as deputy manager in HR department of a large accounting firm.

'I was just going to be there,' Chris said, 'I just wanted to relax a few minutes; how are you feeling?'
'I am okay; I took some pain killers,' Meina replied 'I should have really gone to the party with you.'
'It was not a very good party this year. Besides, you could have gone worse.'
'I know you do not feel comfortable, I mixing up with your office colleagues,' Meina complained.

'No darling, it is not like that at all, Sir Henry thinks you are a fine woman. He, in fact, once said that you can always work for him.'

'Let's go to the bed and talk there.' Meina said.

'Yeah, let's go there.' He got up, finished the last sip of the glass, put it on the table and picked up his jacket.

About half an hour later, Chris and Meina are in their bed, they have been talking about the party. 'Did you meet anyone nice in the party?' Meina asked.

'No I didn't, I was missing you too much,' he said.

'Next time, you take me with you and you will be with a nice person all the time,' she smiled.

'Of course, my darling,' Chris put his hand under her nightie and grabbed her breast. He played with it for a while squeezing her nipples, then he put his other hand on her other breast and kissed her. Before he could really get going, 'I can't, I have my periods.' Meina said it in a meek voice as though it was her fault.

'Oh damn it, why must you have your period on Christmas? Especially when I came early from the party to be with you,' he complained.

'It is not my fault that is how women are made.' They continued to kiss. Chris could almost see Sharon in her; he remembered her sexy body and suddenly felt his erection. Meina also felt it and gently pushed him away. Chris was not deterred, he was quite aroused and wanted to do something.

'When one gate is closed, God opens the other gates,' he whispered in Meina's ears.

'Don't be silly, you know I don't like it. Besides, it makes me almost vomit.' Chris moved his mouth back from her ears and wondered why these stupid Asian girls can't be like European girls? Is it really too much to ask. Kama Sutra, was it really written by Indians? While Chris was thinking all that, Meina, in order to avoid any further physical contact, turns other side. After a few minutes, she almost falls asleep.

Chris is fully awake, he does not know what to do; he knew it was pointless. He cursed Sharon arousing him and to his bad luck that he did not have any 'success' in the party. He could have stayed longer, had anyone like Sharon shown any interest in him. About half an hour later, he started touching himself realising that Meina had fallen asleep. After a short while, when he climaxed thinking about Sharon, he promised himself, one day, he will surely enter those beautiful lips of hers.

About an hour later, since Chris left the Christmas party, Terry and Sharon Hamilton are in a private cab going back to their home. 'Did you have a good time?' asked Terry.
'Oh yes, it was really a good party,' Sharon did not wish to sound too excited about it.
'We changed the caterers this year, the food was excellent.'
'The Champagne wasn't bad either!'
'I noticed you seemed to be a little drunk, dancing so close with Chuck.'
'I had not met him before, he seemed rather nice.'
'Yeah, he is here for a few weeks from New York working on a joint project. We will invite him at our home before he goes back.'
'I think I will keep away from Champagne this time.' Sharon joked.
'No, I don't want you to; I need to get you in the right mood!' Terry looked at her meaningfully.
'I am always in the right mood for you, my darling,' she pulled him towards her, and kissed him.

The cab driver discreetly looks at them in the back mirror and thinks what it is like to be rich and have such a beauty kissing you!

Chapter 2

In the senior partner, Sir Henry Sheldon's office, Chuck is sitting on a small sofa opposite him; a coffee table is in between and has two partly filled coffee cups on it.

'How are you getting along with 'Green Park International Project?' Sir Henry enquired.
'I have made very good progress but will report to you in more details, in a week or so.' Chuck replied.
'How do you find Terry?'
'He is really good, very sharp.'
'Do you get along with him?'
'Yes, in fact, we do get along very well; he has invited me at his home, this weekend.'
'Good, you see Chuck, I run a very tight ship here; it is a good practice.'
'I am sure Sir.'
'You see, I know the main purpose of your visit is 'Green Park International' but I believe you are also looking at our practice. I know Sandy must have asked you to look at the practice carefully.'
Chuck realised, so there is more to him than just an impressive face and a title. 'Not really.' Chuck said.
'I know it is quite natural, your company has been looking to acquire a UK practice, as a base for expansion in Europe.'

'I am sure Sandy would have mentioned to you if that was the case, Chuck did not want to admit. 'Besides, there are more able people in our office to do that.'

'I am sure you are as capable as anyone,' Sir Henry pauses, 'I started this practice alone. I did not have even a chair in my office, since they were going to deliver it in a few days, and I could not wait to be in the office. I worked fifteen hours a day to build this practice, and now it is at such a stage that I find that it can run without me, so I am not worried if a right offer came along. I will be happy to sell it, and spend more time with my family, travel and few other hobbies.'

Chuck was not sure what to say, he was thinking how come did he know the main purpose of his visit? He kept quiet. Sir Henry looked at him meaningfully and brought his head forward and said in a low voice. 'Of course, you will keep this conversation very secret; I do not wish to have any gossips in the office.'

'Sir, I have not agreed with what you have just said, but I promise to keep this conversation between two of us only.' Chuck replied in a serious tone.

'Good then… if you wish to discuss any issues with Green Park International, just let me know.'

'I will… is it possible for me to look at some of the old files of related cases in the filing room? I noticed the filing room is normally kept locked.' Chuck asked.

'Of course, I will let Gordon know, you can access any files you need,' Sir Henry replied.

'Thank you, I will be off then.'

'Good... See you.'

Chuck gets up and leaves Sir Henry's office. Sir Henry sees him going and wonders what a clever dick! Will not agree or deny; why we solicitors are like that!'

In a few minutes, there was a telephone ring. 'Yes Susan?'

'Sir, it is Gordon on the line.'

'Fine, put him through.'
'Gordon here Sir, Chuck is asking to go through some files in the filing room.'
'That's fine, he needs to review some files for his project.'
'Thank you Sir.'

Sir Henry puts the phone down.

Lenny is in a bar in the West End with his girlfriend Joan. They have glasses of gin & tonic in front of them. The bar is pretty full, being near Christmas, they always got busy.

'What's the matter with you? Are you alright?' Joan asked seeing Lenny lost.
'I am alright.'
'My foot… you seem to be lost in some deep thoughts.'
'Not really, there is a lot of work; there are number of things going on in the office, I am working on an urgent investigation.'
'But this is quite a common scenario for you guys?'
'Yes and no... We were expecting to be fairly in Christmas spirit; generally we are not so busy at this time of the year. Everybody is tuned to enjoy, a lot of parties, lunches etc.'
'Ah well, you are an ambitious person, it should be good for your career… no?'

They continue to drink. After a few minutes, when Lenny did not say anything Joan suggested to finish the drink and go. Lenny was all the time thinking about the other night in the filing room with Sharon. Who was the person who saw them and what a cheek to make that kind of remark!
'Can I ask you something as a friend?' Lenny said.
'As a friend!!? And yet, I am your girlfriend!' Joan was sarcastic.

'Sorry, I don't mean that…he hesitates. You see at Christmas party, a friend of mine was rather indiscrete with a senior colleague's wife, and he asked my help... I don't know whether I should get involved.'
'Please tell me and let's see if this fashion designer can help a solicitor!'

Lenny tells her briefly substituting a friend for him.

'I would say the first thing is to find out exactly who saw them, and then the story goes forward.'
'He was not sure, being half drunk did not help.'
'At Christmas parties people do all sorts of thing, the motto is thou shalt forgive, I do not think that person will do anything.'
'But if he did, my friend will probably lose his job.'
'Well, start finding who it was? Who would need to come to the filing room at that time?'
'There is a cloakroom next to the filing room, and toilets.'
'Maybe someone who left early or someone going to the toilet, on tenth floor probably too many people.'
'Yes that's a good idea, it probably someone who left the party early, and collecting the coat from the cloakroom.'
'But why are you worried so much? It is not your problem.'
'I don't know, but if he loses his job, it may affect me, we have been working on this major project together, and his problem will affect me directly.'
'I see.'
Lenny finishes his drink. 'Let me not bore you any longer, let me order another drink, then we will go home, you must listen to this new album I bought.'

Lenny orders waiter another drink while Joan is thinking, why Lenny is lying? Mr Smarty pants thinks that I will not understand. I wonder with whom he has been fucking around; must be someone important, otherwise, he will not be so worried. Anyway, I will settle the score sometime. The waiter brought the drink 'Cheers,' they both said simultaneously.

A few days passed. Sharon worried at the time and the next day, but nothing had happened nor did she hear from Lenny. So she tried to forget what happened at the party night. Terry's behaviour was very normal.

Lenny was very worried. In the office, he decided to go back to the filing room. He stood at the same spot where he and Sharon were at that night, and then he walked to the spot where Chris was standing that night, and had seen their indiscretion. He walked back and forth several times but couldn't work out anything. He left the room even more worried.

Gordon More, the office administrator is in his office at Henry Sheldon LLP, he is in early fifties. He was an ex-army major and had been working in the LLP for the last ten years. He had pleasant manners but one needed to be careful with him because he got into his army mode easily. Sir Henry liked him a lot and he was quite close to him. Lenny enters his office 'Can I speak to you for a minute?'
'Yes sure, come in', Gordon said.
'You know I have been working at this investigation and go to the filing room every now and then.'
'Yes, I know.'
'You see, I was thinking that there are so many files with sensitive information; wouldn't it be dangerous if some outsider had access to the files?'
'The general security of the building is under the control of the 'Security Department' of the office block, they have CCTV and all kind of controls in place, I thought you knew it.'
'Sure I know, but say someone from another floor or even from our own company in the admin or staff support?'
Gordon thinks for a moment wondering why suddenly a solicitor should be so interested in the security. He was not at very senior level like

department managers or general partners. 'Why are you so concerned about it?' Gordon asked.

'The investigation I am working on, has a number of sensitive items and exposures, even in the hands of non-related people, they can cause exposure.' He added 'and you know how Sir Henry is so particular about the reputation of the firm.'

'I do not really like it but I will put your mind at rest,' Gordon explained. 'We got our own CCTV camera fitted in the filing room and many other places; these are not in the control of 'Building Security Department'.'

Lenny did not know that there was CCTV in the filing room. He got a shock but he tried to control his facial expressions. So if Gordon or someone else has seen the party night recording. Gordon looks at him and cannot understand what has affected him! Gordon had not looked at the CCTV records since they were kept as a security precaution, in case there was some incident or report. Otherwise, Lenny probably would have had his P45 the very next day.

'Do you want me to look at any particular day or periods recording? We keep them for one year and then the files get deleted.' Gordon asked.
'No.... I did not wish to waste your time, I just wanted to make sure that we are covered,' Lenny panicked.
Gordon looks at him again meaningfully 'Do you want me to run over the last month or so?'
'No.... please don't, I will just include in my report that we have good security, and adequate internal controls,' Lenny said quickly.
'Good, then we are done.'
'Yes, thank you very much indeed for your help,' Lenny took a sigh of relief.
'See you.'
'Bye.'

Terry Hamilton returned from the office in the evening. He was rather tired. Sharon opened the front door of the house before Terry had a chance to open. 'Hello darling,' Sharon said cheerfully.

'Hello, good to see your smiling face at the door,' he kissed her.

'I knew my dear husband will be home and tired, I have already got your favourite dish, leg of lamb in the oven.'

'Thank you,' as hc entered inside the house. 'I have been working very hard in the office, this urgent project with Chuck and others.'

'How is it going?'

'Okay, but the clients are too busy in their Christmas parties etc.'

They both entered the lounge; he sits on the sofa after putting his briefcase on the side. Sharon rushes to the drink cabinet and pours some whisky and for herself a glass of sherry. Even though, she shows apparent enthusiasm, inside she is worried and wanted to know if anyone spilled the beans in the office or any rumours of the Christmas party. She offers the drink to him, he thanked her and she sits down beside him on the sofa. 'Cheers' he said. While taking a sip of sherry, Sharon asks, 'anything interesting in the office?'

'No, not really; surprisingly we are very busy,' he took a big sip of the whisky.

Sharon did not know how to find out what was going on in the office; does anybody know? Who was the person, was he really Chris? She started thinking. 'Where have you gone? I thought I was the tired one,' Terry looked at her.

'Oh, I am here. I was just thinking about the oven.' She took a sigh of relief thinking, no news is good news. 'I will go to the kitchen while you freshen up.' She got up and went to the kitchen. Terry finished his drink. He was wondering why the clients take things so easy. Christmas season does not mean to be so sloppy and irresponsible. He was still in the office! It is not very easy to switch off. He got up and went to his bedroom to change.

Lenny stayed late in the office while most of his other colleagues had left. He got up from his office and passes Gordon's office. 'Can I help you, I think Gordon has left for the day, Doug (Gordon's assistant) saw Lenny looking closely at Gordon's office.
'Oh... it's nothing I will talk to him tomorrow.'
Doug, who was already late, raised his hand 'good night.' Lenny moved on, he knew he will have to wait another fifteen minutes or so.

About half an hour later, Lenny was in Doug's office. He entered with care so no one sees him. The computer was on since it recorded through a few hidden cameras in the offices. He plays with a few keys but is stuck when the camera recording asked for the password. He looked around at the desk, and tried a couple of the passwords. Seeing it not working, he looks inside one of the drawers. After a few minutes, he sees office manual and on the last page what looked like some passwords. He tried the passwords, on the second attempt; the computer lets him into the system. He scrolls camera 2 outside Sir Henry's office then camera 3 in the filing room.

Lenny slowly scrolls the camera no 3 and watches his colleagues visiting filing room, examining some files taking with them the files or bringing it back. Occasionally, someone sits on the sofa and examines the file over there, sometimes; they take a note on a paper. He scrolled back and saw what he was looking for, the Christmas party night. To his horror he looked at Sharon on the sofa half naked, her pants down, him on top of her, and later he standing and her mouth close to his thighs. He did not really want to watch, it did not look pleasant out of the context. Then he discovers a shadow standing behind the cupboard. Lenny does the close up but still can't see Chris face clearly... Lenny wanted to punch that bastard on the screen.

Lenny stays silent looking around to see if anyone was around. He could not see anyone. It was quiet; most people had left for the day. Lenny does not know what to do. He picks up the phone and rings Sharon on her mobile. She was in the breakfast room with Terry. 'Hi,' she recognised

Lenny's voice. She had deleted his contact details from her mobile to distance from him. 'Sorry I was having dinner with Terry, can I call you later?'

'No it is not necessary, I have seen the camera recording; it was Chris.' Lenny said nervously and without waiting for her to reply he disconnected the phone.

'Who is it darling?' Terry asked.

'Oh not important, it was Linda for a shopping trip to Westfield,' she takes a breath. 'I will call her later.'

They got on with their dinners. Sharon is also worried now; her sixth sense told her that the matter had not gone away. Terry could not help but noticing the change in her colour and worried look at her face.

'Are you alright Sharon?' Terry enquired.

'I think I bit my tongue, nothing serious,' she could not wait to be alone and consider the whole matter again.

They continued with their dinner.

At the office, Lenny looks at the screen again. He thinks hard what should he do? Sharon was an intelligent woman; she could have perhaps given some idea. He pressures his brain, does not quite work, 'shall I damage the computer so that the file is unusable? Maybe it was connected to the server and he could not touch the server, surely backup will have it. After careful consideration, he decides to delete it. Surprisingly, there was no additional password required. He deleted about an hour's coverage. After deleting, he backed up the server overwriting the earlier copy. He looks around, no one was there. He restarts the archived copy and checks that the recording did not show the enjoyable but now the most dreaded hour. He looks around nervously, it was quiet, and no one was around.

Lenny left the office building immediately, not quite sure if he had done the right thing.

Late at night, Sharon is sitting in the lounge watching TV while Terry was reading a file in his bed. Terry looked at the watch it was eleven thirty, he had an early meeting; he felt quite exhausted. All papers, agenda of the meeting, he had read through. He looked tired, he turns the light off. He knew Sharon was watching TV in the lounge. Often when he was doing some office work, she diplomatically left him alone, not to disturb him, and watched TV or listened to the music in the lounge. About fifteen minutes later, Sharon comes to the bedroom and noticed that Terry was already asleep. She, without making any noise goes back to the lounge and rings Lenny.

Lenny was in his bedroom in pyjamas, he also had to attend the early morning meeting with Terry and other colleagues next day. He picks up the phone He hears the low voice of Sharon 'It's me, Sharon, are you okay?'
'Yes, I am a little better,' he was glad she rang. He did want to discuss his earlier 'mission' with some one. 'Can you speak?'
'Yes Terry is sleeping. But I will keep my voice low, can you hear me?'
'Yes, I can... listen..,' he explained to her what he had been doing in the evening in fair detail.
'Are you sure no one saw you?' Sharon asked.
'No, I was very careful,' Lenny replied. 'Do you think it was the right thing to do in the circumstances?
'Yes I suppose.'
'What do you mean, you suppose?' Lenny raised his voice.
'Well these days of cloud storage, there could be several backups.'
Lenny's face shrunk, he did not know so much about computers. 'Shit... I never thought of that!' he confessed. 'God, there is never a perfect

solution! Why Chris needed to be there at that time? I think I am going to confront him.'

Sharon is quiet for a few seconds 'No, don't do anything rash, you must keep cool, let me think,' she pauses a few more seconds. 'Maybe Chris has forgotten he must be a little drunk; maybe he did not recognise us.'

'No, I don't think so. I noticed in the recording that he watched us for a while, so he must have seen us. Besides, he knows you well; he reports to your husband.'

'Anyway, he couldn't prove a thing, especially now the recording was deleted.' Sharon was confused; she was contradicting what she had said earlier about other backups.

'Let's sleep over it and discuss it another time,' Lenny said. No longer calm himself, he wanted to think. He was an ambitious person, sleeping with the boss's wife in the office was definitely a gross misconduct, he knew the result!

'Are you there, Lenny?' Sharon thought he had hung up.

'Yes I am here, I will talk to you another day.'

'Alright; good night.'

'I wish it was a good night… bye.' Lenny disconnected his mobile.

Next day, Chuck was in the filing room. He had been going through some files. He looks around; there was no one else in the filing room. He looks at various filing cabinets on the wall with names of the project/cases written in front. He takes one of the files and sits on the sofa to study it. Then he gets up and moves to a desk and sits on the chair next to it. He started making some notes. After a few minutes, he looks at the ceiling, deep in thoughts. He stares at the ceiling without still thinking, he suddenly noticed that there was a hidden camera on the wall. No one had told him that there was any CCTV there. He was used to all kinds of gadgets and security devices. He gets up and goes near the wall where it joined the ceiling. He pretends that he was looking for some file but actually thinking. He goes behind the cupboard where camera could not see him. In a minute, he takes out a small electronic gadget from his pocket which fires a laser beam towards the camera. After a few seconds, he comes out behind the cupboard and is confident that the camera is no longer working. He starts examining some files very quickly, occasionally taking pictures of some of the documents. He moves fast, he was sure it will take at least an hour before anyone realises that the camera was not working. He continued examining different files.

About an hour later, he takes the relevant case file and sits down on the chair. He was thinking whether to stay or move. Suddenly, Doug Hasketh, a strongly built man in his late twenties, arrived. Chuck noticed him but he continued to be busy in his work. Doug comes closer, Chuck raised his head and smiled 'Hi there, are you okay?' Doug looks at him, trying to appraise him, 'Good morning there', then moves to the cabinet near the wall where the camera was fixed. He pretended that he was looking at the files while trying to understand why in his office the CCTV recoding was showing blank on his screen. He takes a file and walks out of room while Chuck pretended to be busy.

After a few minutes, Chuck leaves the filing room with his working notes etc.

Later that evening, Chuck was in his apartment (he had rented a furnished small apartment for his visit). He was sitting in the lounge; he rings his boss Sandy Gorfield in New York. Sandy picks up the phone 'Hi Chuck, how are you doing?'
Chuck looks at some notes in his file, 'I am good, thanks. I have some news for you. They had another approach about a year ago but after some meetings turned it down.'
Sandy knew exactly what Chuck was talking about, 'any particular reasons?'
'I am not sure, what I gather, the other company was not willing the fees multiple required by Sheldons. Also it seems there were some company culture differences.'

'Good, I am glad to hear it, most helpful. How the other project is going?' Sandy asked.

'Fine, I am working with the team here and we should have the draft report in a week or so.'

'Good work, anything else?'

'No Sandy, I will send you some details by email.'

'Okay bye.'

'Bye.' Chuck pressed the button on his mobile. He seemed relaxed and moved towards the fridge were there was a bottle of Bourbon. He pours it in a glass and takes a big sip.

The same evening, Sharon is sitting in the lounge reading magazine but her mind is not in it. She seemed worried, her mind is troubled what if Chris mentioned the Christmas party night to Terry? What was she going to do? Can she deny it; it would be his word against hers. Can he prove it, yes probably he can; one of the backups can be produced. Should she seek help from Michael (The LLP's IT manger) to delete the incident from all the backups? She will have to explain the whole thing to him, then how she could be sure that he will keep the secret. Can she bribe him? All kinds of thoughts came into her mind. She desperately wanted to talk to someone about it. 'Can't keep it within me, I will explode', she thought.

Sharon gets up and moves out of the lounge to the corridor where there was a large mirror. Terry was in a business dinner which she had declined, so Terry had to go alone. They were going to discuss mostly the business in there. She looks herself in the mirror, her face looked tired; her body still seemed in good shape. She looks at her legs in tight jeans, long smooth legs, quite sexy really, she can use these to get out of any problem, she was sure. But was there a problem? What if Chris had forgotten? She comes back to the lounge with a glass of white wine from the fridge. She takes a big sip, cold wine, tasting good and that relaxed her. She picks up her mobile and rings Meina.

Meina picks up her phone on the other end 'hello.'

'Hi Meina, it is Sharon Hamilton here. How are you?' Sharon said in a cheerful voice.

'Very well, thank you', replied Meina, 'have not heard from you for a long time.'

'Yes I did not see you at the office Christmas party, it was nice,' Sharon still sounding cheerful and friendly.

'I was not well, maybe Chris forgot to mention.' Meina is happy to speak to the wife of her husband's boss. She knew in corporate ladder, contacts and networking was the key.

'No, I did not speak to him, he was hardly there.'

'Yes, he left early because of me…. He really is a good husband,' she said without meaning it.

'Listen we are inviting a few people over dinner next Saturday. Terry and I would love if you and Chris could join us. How are you feeling now?'

'I am well, please wait I will pass you to Chris' she gave the phone to Chris who was sitting nearby.

'Hi Sharon, nice to hear from you; what you guys are celebrating?'

'Oh, nothing, we invited a few friends and would like you to join us,' she said, the friendly tone with Meina, had gone.

'I am surprised you remember me, have not been to many parties you held before!' Chris was slightly sarcastic.

'Well we remember you now, we don't really invite all the friends and colleagues at the same time,' she replied ignoring his sarcasm.

Chris knew he could twist her; he was carrying such a big secret. In the past, she had always declined his advances, he really fancied her. Suddenly, the picture of the party came into his mind, he could remember beautiful body but unfortunately it was Lenny and not he with her.

'Are you there Chris?' Sharon asked.

'Oh so sorry, I was thinking if we had any prior engagement', he looked at Meina who with her hand gesture points that they did not have any other engagements. 'We would love to come, thanks Sharon.' Chris replied with formal politeness.

'Good, we are looking forward to seeing you, bye.'

'Bye.' Chris pressed the mobile button.

Chris and Lenny are in a pub in Knightsbridge. It's a typical classic English pub with Mahogany wood work, large beautiful mirrors, glasswork, and luxurious chairs. At the bar there were three good looking bartenders, two female and one male. The pub is not yet crowded being still early in the evening, Chris and Lenny having just arrived and their drinks in front of them.

Chris knew what Lenny wanted to talk. Lenny had asked him in the office if they could just have a casual drink in the pub. They were not very friendly but knew each other well and socialised in office do's. Chris looks at Lenny and picks up his glass of beer 'Cheers'. Lenny picks up his glass but seemed to be in deep thoughts trying to collect how he was going to start the conversation. 'Cheers' he said in a low voice. Chris looks at him with piercing eyes 'so what did you want to discuss? I hope it is not this bloody 'Green Park International'. I am so tired of discussing it over and over again.' He took another big sip from his glass. Lenny does not like the way he looked at him but could not quite read the spark of hostility in his eyes. 'You left in the Christmas party early? How is Meina?' Chris' gaze becomes a little more friendly when Lenny talked about his wife. 'She is alright now. I think it was flu, she tends to get every year in December.'
'That's good.' Lenny goes back quiet again.
'Did you have a good time?' asked Chris not knowing if Lenny knew that he had seen him and Sharon in the filing room.
'Yes, I did, there were a lot of people' Chris mustered courage. 'Look Chris, I do not wish to beat about the bush, you are too smart for that; I had a special agenda for this meeting.' He takes a big sip of beer from his glass. 'You see Chris, at Christmas parties people often forget what they are doing; after all it is a festive period.'

Chris knew where has was coming from. 'Of course, everyone has a right to unwind and enjoy; after all Christmas comes once a year,' he tried to sound casual.

Lenny now looks at his face carefully reading his thoughts. 'Chris that day… I and Sharon got a little drunk and were carried away,' he muttered.

'Well that's alright, you are a bachelor still and she is a very liberated woman, I am glad you shared your secret with me!' He said in a matter of fact voice as though it was not important at all.

Lenny decided not to talk diplomatically anymore and said bluntly.

'When we were in the filing room thinking we were alone and far from the party, someone walked in and saw us'.

'What is has got to do with me?' Chris decided to play with him.

Look Chris we are not children, nor in the office looking at client's case; we both knew it was you.' Lenny looked at him aggressively remembering that the son of a bitch could have kept quiet and not given them a shock with his remark.

Chris is quiet for a few moments, he knew that he was not discrete about it and somehow wanted to punish Sharon for her past indifference to him. Chris looks at Lenny without any emotion even though; he felt the hostility in his voice. 'Sorry Lenny, I am not saying that it was me or not, but seeing you in your supposed indulgence, is it my fault?' Chris remarked.

'No it is not… except that you could have kept quiet and be discrete about it.' Lenny complained.

Chris thinks for a minute, takes another sip from his glass and looks around. 'Forgive me, if you have been fucking that woman and not careful why is it that others should turn a blind eye. You were not quite examining a client's case file, were you? But fucking a woman who happens to be my boss's wife,' he exploded.

Lenny got angry with his remarks but controls himself; he also looks around to see if anyone was listening to their conversation. 'We know it was you, first of all, I would like you to admit it, and secondly, promise me that you never saw it, it never happened.' Lenny almost warned him. 'Look Lenny, you are not in a position to ask me what I should or shouldn't do; I do not owe you anything or to Sharon. In fact, she has been rather unpleasant to me in the past,' he said in a cool voice ignoring his warning.

'What unpleasant she has been with you, if she slept with me, it does not mean that she is going to screw with every Tom, Dick and Harry.' Lenny said quickly. 'Chris, we do not punish people just because they have been indifferent or ignore one's sexual advances, she is really a nice woman.' Lenny added.

'What a presumption! Who told you that I made any sexual advances to her? What gives you the right to describe me as anyone, I belong to the same establishment, senior than you, in the rank, perhaps not as good looking as you but smart enough.' Chris said angrily.

'I know it is a case of sour grapes.' Lenny also replied angrily.

'Sorry Lenny, instead of trying to reason it out you are behaving like an idiot, did I say that I was going to put it on the office board that our dear colleague Mr Lenny Crowe has been screwing our department manger's wife; he should be promoted for this achievement,' he retorted.

Lenny realised that he has not been arguing well and tried to cool him down. 'I think you are getting all upset for nothing, I am sure you are a good looking and smart person. You are married. She is also married, besides, what is it going to cost you to promise that you will forget it, please Chris.' Lenny pleaded.

Chris took another sip from his glass and gets up. 'You have upset me unnecessarily but because you are my office colleague, I will consider what you said.' He leaves the pub without saying anything further.

Lenny wanted to say something but Chris had already gone. He thinks for couple of minutes, sees half-filled glass of Chris who had not finished his drink, picks his own glass and drinks the remaining beer in one gulp. He rings Sharon on his mobile.

'Hi, Lenny,' he heard Sharon's beautiful voice.

'Hi Sharon, I had a meeting with Chris. He was really unpleasant. He claimed that you have not been very nice to him in the past, so he cannot promise to keep quiet.' Lenny explained.

'I have not been unpleasant with him. I am not attracted by all men. You do not know him well, he is a slimy bastard. I am sure he is not going to keep quiet.' Sharon became angry.

'Sorry Sharon, I did not mean to upset you but I do not know what to do? I am sure if Terry learns about it, I will get fired and even if not, he is the department manager, it is never going to work. Maybe, I should look for another job.'

Sharon agreed with him in her heart but he sounded so worried, she forgot her own problems and tried to console him. 'Lenny, Chris is a professional person just like you, he is also your colleague, I am sure he will be discrete.'

'No Sharon, the way he reacted and the way he left, it does not sound very promising.'

'Don't worry too much, I will see you at the dinner, will think of something, let's put our heads together some time.'

'Do you think I should come to the dinner? Wouldn't it be better to stay low?' Lenny asked.

'On the contrary, my darling, it will prove you have something to hide, I will come if I were you,' Sharon advised him.

'Okay, if you say so.'

'Bye.'

'Bye, see you.'

Chapter 3

In a tree lined street in Mill Hill, a good residential street of North
London, there is a dinner party. The houses in the street are mostly
detached and although not very big, are very expensive since the street is
one of the exclusive pocket of this part of London. In front of Terry
Hamilton's house, there is a good size lawn, and a garage on one side of
the lawn. In front of the garage, a number of cars were parked from
Bentleys to BMW's; some cars were parked in the street.

Inside the well-furnished house, in the lounge which is quite spacious, the
party is going on. In adjoining dining room, the table is laid out with all
kinds of snacks and drinks. Most people are drinking cocktails, there is a
hired help called Rebecca Strings who is assisting in serving the drinks
and canapes to the guests. Some guests were standing while others were
sitting on the sofa and the chairs.

Sharon Hamilton is wearing a tight mid-size skirt, in spite of the size of
the skirt; one could see her beautiful legs. She is in her early thirties and
is really a beautiful woman. Her hair is done, and the silk shirt is open in
front just enough for people to see a glimpse of her beautiful breast and
wonder what is would be like to see them in full, and indeed to touch
them! She is a director of an art gallery. She visited the gallery about
three times a week normally unless there were some special functions or
presentation or some artist's work displayed. She would attend all the
special events. Her young son Max, who is ten years old, was in a private
boarding school.

Sharon is talking to Meina who is wearing a very tight silk sari, and a small blouse which covers her breasts but shows bulk of her tummy while the tight sari shows her shapely bottom. She has a light brown complexion. She is in her mid to late twenties. Next to her is Linda Hammond, a friend of Sharon, a woman also in her mid- thirties dressed in a smart dress. All three are busy in talking while others, men and women in small groups are busy discussing from office business to the current politics.

Rebecca comes with a tray containing glasses of cocktails and Champagne, Linda puts back her empty cocktail glass and picks up another one. Sharon does not want to drink too much, she knew with drinks she gets carried away! Linda teases Sharon 'I see you are keeping sobers, so that you do not spill any beans or just saving on the drinks in current financial climate?'
Sharon smiles 'Alas I have nothing to disclose, a simple house wife with a very routine life.'
Meina also smiles. 'We know how routine you are, with all the office parties, social engagement, exhibitions and meeting with those wonderful artists.'
'It has been very long time since I met anybody really interesting; tell me how the accounting world is doing?' Sharon replied.
'You know the accountants, boring like hell, that's why I married a solicitor......well it is not any better.'
'All the professional people are the same really, estate agents aren't any better!' Linda added.

While they were talking, Sharon noticed Sir Henry and Pamela Sheldon entering the room; she immediately excuses herself and goes to greet them. At the same time, Terry who was standing in a small group also excuses himself and walks quickly to greet Sir Henry and Pamela. 'Good evening Sir Henry,' said Sharon. 'Good evening,' he kissed on her both cheeks while Terry does the same on Pamela's cheeks. Sir Henry and Terry shake hands. 'I see the party is going well,' remarked Sir Henry. 'Yes Sir, a lot of people are here from the office.' Terry said. 'What would you like?' while walking towards a small group. 'A little whisky on the rocks will do,' replied Sir Henry.

'Pamela for you?' Terry asked.

'Champagne please, if some left.' Pamela smiled.

'Oh dozens of bottles, we are never short of Champagne in this house.' Terry looked teasingly at Sharon. Sharon smiled but did not say anything. Terry went to fetch the drinks while Sir Henry, Pamela and Sharon joined the group.

The party continued, the food was served in the dining room, some standing and some sitting in the lounge which was quite spacious. One side of the lounge was provided for the dancing. In background, the instrumental music played. After a short while, Rebecca put the dancing track on the stereo and a few people started dancing.

In a corner, Chris Sneale, Meina Sneale and few other people were standing and talking. Lenny looked at Meina from distance, she really looked beautiful. He wondered how come Chris managed to get such a pretty woman as his wife. He wanted to ask her for a dance but remembering the unpleasant meeting with Chris a few days ago, he decided against it. Instead he went to Linda and asked her. 'May I?'

'Oh yes please, I thought no one is going to ask me.' Linda said jokingly.

'I am sure a lot of people want to but do not dare.'

'Am I so frightening?'

'No my dear, you look so beautiful and elegant!'

'Oh go on... flattery will get you everywhere.'

'No I mean it; you really are such an impressive person.' Lenny knew how to treat the ladies.

'Wonderful, she came close to him; do continue!' She whispered.

Lenny tightened his grip. The record was playing 'This girl is on fire'.

'Are you on fire?'

'Yes I am, how did you know?' her hands slipped to his bottom for a few seconds. Lenny could feel her breast and her thighs often touching his. She was on fire alright, he thought.

From the distance Chris noticed Lenny dancing close to Linda. That son of a bitch really is lucky, when he noticed that they were so close to each other. I am sure soon he is going to take her to the bedroom upstairs. Suddenly, he heard a voice in American accent' Mam, may I?' he heard Chuck asking Meina for a dance.

'With pleasure,' and Meina was gone with Chuck.

'We haven't met before,' said Meina.

'No, I am from the New York office, here for a few weeks on a joint project.' Chuck replied. 'May I say you look really lovely in this sa...dress.'

'Thank you, it is called sari.' Meina looked at him closely. He was tall, well-built man in his late thirties/early forties with piercing eyes like he sees through the people.

They continued to dance and talk. A number of people were dancing mostly with other people's wives or single women.

It is almost midnight and the party is in full swing. Suddenly, the music stopped and there was the sound of a spoon against a glass. It was Terry: 'Sorry to disturb you guys but I and Sharon would like to thank you all for coming. It has been a real pleasure. I interrupted the party to make a special announcement. Firstly, some of you might not have met Chuck Orcel. He is from our New York office, this party was a way to introduce him to all friends, and seeing the way he is mixing I would say it has been successful. Until today, I did not know that among other qualities, he is such a good dancer.' Chuck looks around with a small bow of his head, everybody looks at him. Terry continued, 'it is my great pleasure, ladies and gentlemen to inform you that Sir Henry has been short listed for the City's Lord Mayor Position for the next year. May I congratulate him on behalf of all of us.'

Everybody claps. Sir Henry said 'thank you,' he decided not to say anything further.

'May I propose a toast for Sir Henry' Terry said proudly, and raised his glasses; all others raised their glass 'to Sir Henry.' They all said together.

'Now ladies and gentlemen please continue, Sharon and I are night birds, so please do continue'. Terry did not want the party to lose its momentum. He takes his wife to the dance floor while Rebecca puts some slow rhythm music on.

A few minutes later, Chris was dancing with Sharon. She did not really want to but wanted to cool things. She and Lenny intentionally had avoided each other except casual greetings; besides, Lenny seemed quite 'busy' with Linda. Sharon wondered if he did not bring his girlfriend intentionally. Chris said, 'I am so sorry about the other day,' he did not know that Lenny had relayed his meeting to her in detail. Sharon is quiet for a few moments then replied, 'let's enjoy the evening, and not talk about it.' Chris held her a little close, Sharon did not object. 'Meina really looks nice today.' Sharon remarked. 'Yes, she does, she has recovered from her flu.' Chris also looked at Meina who was with Chuck.

Terry invited Rebecca for a dance and they join others on the floor on a romantic slow rhythm song. He holds her tight; he had seen how others were taking 'advantage' of the evening. Rebecca thought he was a bit drunk since he had never shown any closeness before; she looks at him into his eyes but couldn't read anything. He is too clever, never gives anything away, she thought. She could feel him all over her. She neither encouraged him nor discouraged him. After couple of minutes, she felt his hands moving from her back to her bottom, she feels worried in case someone sees them, particularly, Sharon but then everybody was busy in their own things. No one had really time to see what others were doing. She noticed a lot of couples very close. Terry moved his hands from her bottom to her back and pulls her closer. The drinks and atmosphere affects Rebecca and her young blood moves faster in her veins. She also starts moving her hands on his body, dancing close so that they could feel each other. Rebecca had to hold Terry's hand tight when she felt that it was probing in between her thighs after falling from her breast, not because she did not like it but with the fear that someone will notice it. Solicitors are no different than any other men! She concluded.

The house, in a street going uphill in Mill Hill, continued to bring joy to a number of solicitors and their 'partners' for the evening.

A few days later, Chuck is in the office of Doug Hasketh, he wanted to see the computer recording to do his secret reports on the operations of Henry Sheldon LLP. Gordon Moore and Dough Hasketh had gone for the day. He takes out his key ring from his pocket and with a small torch in it, he discretely aims it on the room all round and looks at the torch side a digital display, something which identifies hidden cameras in the room. Immediately, he presses a button and the laser beam light burns wire of the hidden camera; and the CCTV stops recording. He sits down on the computer and goes through the cameras, all four of them. He noticed in the recording, he entering Doug's office and taking something out of his pocket. He immediately put a USB device in the computer which allows him to enter into the system. He deletes a few minutes recording which showed his entrance to that room. After that, he goes through all the cameras and sees it functioning well, everything getting recorded. The filing room camera which he had rendered useless had been replaced. He was impressed with the system which seemed quite efficient. He rolled the filing room camera back and suddenly realised that some data had been deleted. Chuck looks around carefully to make sure no one was there close by.

Chuck was wondering why anyone should delete the data from the filing room's camera recording. There were a number of confidential files therein and quite a lot of sensitive information of high profile cases. Is the office on radar, police or M15 on it, keeping an eye on some client's agents, examining files for their benefit? The LLP also acted in M&A activity. He went through the filing room recording in fast mode, noticing and recognising the faces of staff and partners of the LLP. He did not find anything, no trespasses or compromise on security. He thinks for a while then he moves to the backups which were offsite but could be reached from that computer.

Chuck's face showed a lot of surprise when in the backup, he finds that the deleted area was the Christmas party; he examined for a few minutes the sexual activity of Sharon and Lenny. The pictures were clear; in spite of his initial shock he could not help admiring the beautiful body of Sharon. I need to lay this broad, he resolved in his mind. Then his eyebrows widened when he noticed that in the room behind the shelf, someone was watching. He goes back in slow speed and noticed that the shadow is there for quite a few minutes, and before leaving, comes out from behind the shelf in front of surprised couple. The picture of the person was not clear, after watching a few times, and in spite of his Agency training, he could not work out who it was? There were a number of solicitors and supporting staff who could foot the bill.

Was it Terry following his wife and watching her misbehaviour or did he want to get rid of her and was looking for an evidence? Who deleted the file? He had no problem in recognising Sharon and Lenny. Was it Terry who after learning the incident asked Doug to delete it, so there is no embarrassment in the office? Or someone else, or maybe Gordon who did not want to have a scandal in the office; everyone knew that Terry was very close to Sir Henry. Or is it Lenny who must have known that someone caught him red handed and wanted to delete the proof.

It was not long before Chuck examined the camera recording of Doug's office showing Lenny sitting in Doug's computer. But who was in the shadow? He continued to wonder in his mind.

Sharon was in the lounge of her home. She was waiting for Terry to come home. It was nearly time for him to come back. She put the magazine down from her hand to the table and starts thinking. Their party was a huge success, everybody seemed to have enjoyed. Lenny had intentionally ignored her but then he was also busy with Linda. What a sexy man, no one can keep her hands away from his body, she thought. Pamela had thanked her the following day for a wonderful party even though, she and Sir Henry had left a little after midnight. She danced with Chris but could not work out whether he was going to tell Terry about it. Of course, that will put him in the good books of Terry who thought Chris was a bloody good lawyer. Chuck seemed to be smitten by Meina, he had spent quite a lot of time with her that night; she noticed they danced quite close but then everybody was taking liberties, oblivious that there were others in the room and that some of their partners were the wives of others who were also present in the party. Then she remembered Terry, falling all over Rebecca, they both were of the same kind, she thought. They can't keep their hands away from their partners when a few bubblies are parked inside their tummies. Should she not invite in future Rebecca? She wondered. She stands up and goes in front of the mirror and looks at herself. She was far prettier to be worried about Rebecca who only had young age in her favour. She goes to the fridge in the kitchen and takes a glass of white wine and goes back to the lounge.

After a few minutes, she picks up the daily newspaper and start reading it. The paper was full of gossips, ex-wives stories whose husbands had hidden their wealth from their wives and as a result, smaller settlements were awarded in divorce to their wives. Her mind moved from it to the lingering threat of Chris talking to Terry about Christmas party. How could she delete that memory from Chris's mind? She knew he was always lusting after her. Maybe she should sleep with him and let someone else see it. That will shut him up! Or it would expand her worries? Maybe she should come clean with Terry and admit everything; but how Terry was going to react, he loved her too much but jealousy had no bounds. Maybe she should sleep with Chris just once to shut him up for ever. In spite of Chris having average looks, she could not imagine sleeping with him, but then what medicine is tasty! Suddenly, she heard the noise at the door. Terry was entering the house. She rushed to greet him. 'Hello darling, you are a bit late?'

'Yes, there was a usual signal failure in the tube.' Terry complained. He kissed her lightly on her lips.

Sharon looks at him with seducing eyes. 'Let me get you some cold wine to put you in the right mood,' she walked to the kitchen.

Next day, Chuck is in the office of Gordon Moore, the office manager. They have been discussing the project he was working on and access to the files. He pointed out that there were a number of sensitive files over there, and no apparent security. Particularly, the Green Park International project was very confidential and had a number of implications in the wrong hands, not to mention the problem it could cause with Financial Conduct Authority.

'Why is it that everyone seems to be so concerned about the security?' Gordon said in irritable voice.

'Well, I have already explained that certain information, even in the hands of the colleagues who were not involved in the project, is dangerous and any leak could cause major embarrassment for the LLP,' he waits, 'and it might even trigger a full blown investigation.' Chuck warned in serious tone.

'Yes I understand but only the other day I had similar conversation with Lenny, who I believe is working with you on this project.' Gordon replied.

'Yes of course, he is; but I did not discuss the filing room security with him. You are the office manager and in charge of the office security.'

Gordon thinks briefly, he can't understand, there has never been any instance or compromise on the office security since he had been with the LLP. 'To put your mind at ease, I would like to point out that there has never been an incident or any leak or indeed any foul play in our office since I have been here,' he said proudly.

'Yes sir, I am fully aware that you are a major, and I am sure anyone would think twice before they do anything wrong!'

Gordon feels even more proud, so he knows that I am not just an ordinary office manager; very few people knew that he was also in military police for a while. 'Chuck, the filing room is really secure, you needn't worry, but let me tell you something which is not known to the staff, there is a hidden camera and everything gets recorded and monitored.'

'That is excellent sir, do you go through the recording yourself?'

'No it is my assistant Doug,' he paused, 'you met him, no?'

'Yes I did; thanks. Does he report everything to you if he finds anything questionable?'

'There has not been anything serious since last year. However, one day recently, we had the malfunction of the cameras but it was fixed quickly.'

'That's very good, but may I request you to ask Doug to go through the filing room recording, at least since the time I have been here, working on the "Green Park International"; this will really put my mind at ease,' he pleaded with apparent sincerity.

'No problems, Chuck, you guys in States are obsessed with security!' Gordon smiled.

'Thank you sir, really appreciate it.' Chuck gets up.

'See you.' Gordon said.

'See you.' Chuck leaves his office.

Chapter 4

In the human resources office, Anwar Rampuri is reading a report. He is in his late forties, a qualified solicitor who headed the human resources department of the LLP, responsible for recruitment, remuneration and staff development etc. He is one of the general partners of the LLP, and reported directly to Sir Henry.

After a few minutes, he takes his glasses off. In the report Gordon Moore has described the details of the misconduct of Lenny Crowe, the rising star of the young solicitors of the firm. He is thinking why anyone should destroy his career to get involved in such a stupid way, and instead of coming clean and apologising, does even more stupid thing to upset the security department and compromise LLP's security. He liked Lenny as he liked many others in the firm, but in the report Gordon had requested him to be sacked with immediate effect. A copy of the report was CC'd to Sir Henry and Lenny's department manager, Terry Hamilton. He picks up the phone and rings Terry.
'Hi Anwar,' Terry replied.
'Can I come and see you about Lenny? You have seen Gordon's report?'
Terry was busy but the matter was important and urgent. 'Sure, you want to come now or shall I come to you?'
'I will be there in a few seconds.' Anwar put the phone down.

Shortly afterward, Anwar walks into the office of Terry. He closed the door behind him carefully. Terry gets up and shakes hand with him, 'Would you like a coffee or something?' Terry asked.
'No thanks, I just had a coffee.'

They discussed Gordon's report. Terry already had an interview with Lenny the day before, and had told him that the matter was out of his hands, and that the final decision rested with Sir Henry and Anwar.
'You have read the report, I believe you had a meeting with Lenny, 'so what is your final decision?' asked Anwar.
'I like Lenny; I think he has a good future with the firm.'
'Yeah, I thought he was really doing well; he had a good comment in the press only recently.'
'But we cannot ignore this serious breach of trust and unprofessional behaviour, the LLP would become a joke, Sir Henry and I both discussed it, he was not happy at all. He has to go.' Terry said it in a serious voice.
'Gordon is really mad at him; he would have loved to fire Lenny himself on the spot.' Anwar remarked.
'Well, that is his military background; he has no jurisdiction on the professional staff.'
'Absolutely right...., does Lenny know where he stands?'
'Yes, I believe so; I had a feeling he knew that he was a goner; the only question was about his reference...obviously, he does not want the real reasons to be disclosed.'
'It is not in our interest to disclose the real reasons outside these walls.'
Anwar stopped for a few seconds, 'I will meet him later today and will work out a solution.'
'That's fine; do let me know if you need any assistance.'
'Is there any reason to delay his departure if he decides to go immediately?' Anwar asked.
'No, the projects he is working are all covered; we got another person to take over his duties in the main project, by adding another person to expedite the work.' Terry emphasised the word 'expedite'.

They both are quiet for a few moments.

'Do you know who was the girl involved?' Terry asked.

'I have no idea, Gordon will not disclose it… it has to be one of those young fillies (referring to young secretaries in the office).'

'I also think so… maybe we should send out a memo about the office behaviour.'

'I think it is already covered in the office manual. I suggest we do nothing…more gossips in the office is not really needed!' Anwar advised Terry.

'Yes, you are right.'

'Alright then, I will deal with this matter from here onward.' Anwar declared.

'Good luck!' Terry said.

Anwar got up and left the office devising his next step.

Gordon is in his office. He had confronted Lenny before writing the report. He had let him know in no uncertain terms that his behaviour deserved dismissal on the spot, but that the decision was in the hands of Sir Henry and Anwar. He had screamed at his assistant Doug, for not doing his job properly, not watching the recording periodically, and advising him. He was also cross with Doug for leaving his password in the desk which was unlocked. Doug had apologised and was glad that he was not fired immediately. However, he was put on three months written warning that any further delinquency will result in immediate dismissal without any notice or pay. Gordon also had got the cameras replaced, the ones which will not burn easily on the change of voltage which burned the wire and caused the cameras to malfunction, (he did not know who was responsible for its failure?). He gets up and goes to adjoining office where Doug was sitting; he was watching the screen very carefully. Since the 'episode' he did not want to take his eyes off the screen.

Doug sees Gordon entering the office, he sits even more attentively.
'Doug, my confidential report has been with Sir Henry, Terry and Anwar.
You have not seen it, apart from Lenny and Chuck's names, there are no
other names on it…. yes, your name is also in it.' Gordon almost
whispered in a serious tone.'
'Yes Gordon, I understand, mum's the word.' Dough said it obediently.
'You know the lady concerned?'
'Yes, I do, but I can assure you my lips are sealed.'
'Doug, I have worked for this firm for many years… It is a good firm and
above all they really are fair…. I do not want that some silly little things
spoil the reputation of the firm, we work for government departments
often…. Do you understand?'
'Gordon, I can assure you that I really do understand. Once more my
apologies for this oversight, I think it was Christmas season and the party
spirit.'
'Okay, if Terry knew it was his wife, I do not know what would have
happened.' Gordon convinced that Doug was going to be discrete about
it. He had already asked the IT manager to record Doug's telephone
conversation until further notice.
'It is just as well you did not mention it, I have already got all the backup
copies deleting the 'episode'.' Doug assured him.
'Did you work out who was the person in the shadow?'
'No, it could be anyone, looking by the size of it. A number of people
will fit the description… anyway, whosoever it was; there has not been
even a whisper in the office about it.'
'Maybe someone walked in and realised what was going on and decided
to forget. Maybe that person was drunk himself.'
'Yes maybe, but I will keep my ears to the ground, and will report to you
if I hear anything.'
'Fine….. How new cameras are working?' Gordon asked.
'They seem to be a lot better, now there will be no more shadows, even in
dark, the pictures will come clear.' He looked at Gordon meaningfully.
'Don't look for shadows man, get on with it.' Gordon said it in a mocking
anger while getting up from the chair to leave.

Doug admired his loyalty to the firm, and took a sigh of relief again; he was so close to being fired.

In the afternoon, there is a meeting in the office of the HR Director Anwar. There is a small round table in the office with a few chairs. Three of these were occupied by Lenny, Gordon and Anwar. The office door is tightly shut; Anwar had made sure that his secretary, who was in the front of his office in an enclosed area with his own office, was not to let anyone disturb the meeting. There were some papers on the table in front of them.

Anwar's face is very matter of facts, not giving signs of any emotions; Gordon's face showing some unpleasantness while Lenny looked visibly upset. Lenny who had already apologised to Gordon and Terry said, 'I repeat I am really sorry, it was just a party thing, I got carried away.'
Anwar who liked Lenny, had no real choice in the matter, both Terry and Sir Henry had almost decided. 'Lenny, I understand we have been young as well but we cannot compromise the integrity of the firm.'
Before Lenny could say anything Gordon interrupted, 'it is more to do with deleting the recording to hide what you had done; you know this compromised firm's controls and exposed it.'
Lenny is quiet for a few moments; he was surprised that so far neither Anwar nor Gordon had mentioned Sharon. I admit, it was stupid of me to do that but I can assure you there was never any intention to expose the firm.'
'Lenny, we do not know who was with you in the filing room that night', he looks at Gordon who also nods with his head, 'the file was deleted and Doug also deleted the backups…. What I will say to you that the matter has been carefully considered by myself, Terry and Sir Henry… I really do not have any choice but to ask you to resign.' Anwar said it thoughtfully.
'In old days, you would have been given your P45 the very same day!' Gordon added.

Lenny is quiet; it did not come as a surprise to him, 'alright when do you want me to leave?' He asked in a desperate voice.

'I will go through the details with you.' Anwar looks at Gordon who understood.

'Well, if you do not need me, I will be off.' Gordon got up.

'Thanks Gordon, I will call you if needed.'

'I will be in my office for another hour then I have to attend another meeting.' Gordon left the office.

Lenny and Anwar looked at each other. 'Before we go any further, I would like to advise you that whoever that person was with you that night, you should forget it, I hope this sad story will finish here.' Anwar said.

Lenny thought how come no one knows that it was my boss's wife, Sharon. 'I was too drunk to remember it myself,' he controlled himself so that he does not slip.

'Okay, that's fine.' Anwar took a sip from the glass in front of the table. Lenny does the same.

Anwar thought for a minute, he wanted to make the process less painful for Lenny. He was sorry; he always thought Lenny will do really well in the firm. 'Look Lenny, I think you resign immediately; you have three months' notice, you can decide the actual date of leaving. I will expect it to be within weeks and not in months. We will pay the balance of your notice period.'

'But what about the reference, what would be written officially in the records?'

'You can write in your resignation letter that you wish to pursue a better opportunity elsewhere or that you were going overseas. The firm's policy is to confirm the period of employment, we generally do not give any reference.'

'But surely, any new employer would like to know; besides I do not have any jobs lined up.' Lenny pleaded.

Anwar looked at Lenny, his upset and sad face. He is sympathetic, 'we will only give the period of employment; if someone enquires about you, it will be Terry who they will talk, I can assure you he really likes you and is very sorry to see you go.'

'So the matter was decided completely before.' Lenny complained.
'You know this type of decisions are not taken lightly, all consultations
have been done, and the approval of Sir Henry himself.'
'I see.'
'In the official records, it will be written that you left voluntarily and
that's what all the office will be told, it is now up to you to keep the right
attitude and be very diplomatic about it.' Anwar advised. 'I will also have
a word with Terry that your indiscretion is not mentioned to outsiders but
only your good work.' Anwar's face showed first time the slight smile.

Lenny is relieved; what a diplomatic person, he is firing me, yet he makes
me feel as though he is doing me a great favour. In spite of his anger, he
could not dislike Anwar. 'So that's it?' He asked Anwar.
'There are some small details, you need to see Terry and make sure all
files, work etc are in place, no loose ends, handover the project work to
Chin… you got "Exit Form", complete it, and hand over the firm's
mobile, iPad, laptop and credit card and anything else which belongs to
the firm.'
'Yes, I know the procedure.' Lenny said in a flat voice.
'Lenny, let this episode be a lesson to you, you are a young man, bright
smart; you can start your career again.' Anwar sounded sincere.
'Thanks, I will try my best… you will have the resignation letter at your
desk tomorrow morning.' Lenny got up.
Anwar also got up and extended his hand. They shook hands. Lenny left
Anwar's office taking his papers with him not really knowing exactly
what he was expecting.

A few minutes later, Anwar was keeping the cassette recording of his
meeting with Lenny in a locked cabinet in his office. He made some
notes and attached it with Gordon's report and put it in Lenny's personnel
file. He picked up the phone and rang Terry and summarised his
interview with Lenny. How could I find who was the girl that night? He

kept on thinking. Suddenly, there was a call from Mendy that Sir Henry wanted to see him. He left the office immediately.

In the evening, Terry and Sharon were sitting in the lounge. Sharon was watching TV while Terry was reading the Financial Times. Terry's mind was not in paper, he could not stop thinking about the office. It is not every day someone gets fired and in such unusual circumstances. He needed to speak. In the office, he had kept absolutely quiet about it. He did not explain to Chin why he was added in 'Green Park International' project, only, that Lenny was going to be away for a while. Chin did not ask many questions, he was glad to be in the project with very visible career prospects, working along with Chuck and others, and one of the most important persons in the firm, Terry.

After a few minutes, Terry could not put his office hat away. He put his newspaper down and looked at the pretty woman sitting next to him. She is as beautiful inside as she is outside, a pleasure to be with; all eyes looking at her when they attended a party. How lucky has he been: a beautiful wife, an impressive house in an exclusive part of a good suburb, excellent job, good visibility in the City and plenty of money. He thanked God for His kindness.

'What are you looking at?' Sharon noticed that he was looking at her, even though; his mind seemed to be thinking something different.
'Oh nothing, it is just the office thing.'
I know it is very difficult for you to switch off…anything special, don't tell me you are going to be promoted again!'
'No I am already head of the department "Commercial and Financial Services" … and Sir Henry is not yet retiring.'
'I bet your bonus has been declared and you don't know how to spend it!' Sharon joked.
'No… relax; I am going to tell you.' Terry said it with a mock irritation, but his face was serious. 'Let me get you a drink.' Sharon gets up and

poured some scotch in two crystal glasses from the decorative cupboard in the lounge. 'Here you are my darling, now you can pour your heart out!' She comes back with the glasses, giving him one.

'Thanks I needed it.' Terry took a big sip.

'Today Lenny was fired in the office.' Terry said it in a flat voice. Sharon nearly dropped her glass; she was shocked. Terry had never mentioned anything that there were any problems in the office. She manged to stay cool and said to him in a matter of fact voice, 'that is a surprise; I thought he was a rising star in your firm!'

'Yes, he was.' Terry said, and stayed quiet for a while.

Sharon's mood suddenly changed. 'God no; it has not happened,' she thought in her mind. Terry noticed sudden change of her mood and wonders why should she be so shocked? He looked at her, 'Anwar and I know about it. He was involved in a gross misconduct.'

Sharon's face darkened further. She almost felt she was going to faint. She takes a big sip of the scotch and controls her nerves 'I am all ears,' she said quietly.

'I hope you will keep it to yourself.' Terry said.

Sharon's mind ran with a speed. Oh God, no; Chris has not done it, that idiot is so unpredictable, even though, she was 'nice' with him in the dinner party. If he had done, then Terry would have been in a rage, he wouldn't have kept so cool like that. It is almost two hours since he got back. She thinks fast and tries to analyse the position; so Terry does not know. Then why Lenny was fired? Her mind comes to a full stop.

Terry was noticing the changes in her, even though, she tried to look as normal as before, 'where have you gone my dear wife!' asked Terry.

'Oh, nothing, you still do not believe that I can keep a secret. I am so used to your office gossips. Besides, I hardly talk to anyone from your office except sometimes to Meina,' she tried to keep her cool.

'Of course, my darling, I would have never spoken to you about the office things if I knew that you could not keep it to yourself.'

Sharon tries not to show her impatience and worries but she was sure that he did not know about the Christmas party saga. She keeps quiet.

'You see Lenny had been indiscrete at the office Christmas party', Terry was not looking at her otherwise, he would have seen the change of colour on Sharon's face, 'then he tried to delete the recording in Doug's office.'

'What exactly did he do in the office party?' Sharon said, she knew very well about both activities but she tried to sound as being startled.

'He was with some girl; apparently, they both were drunk and they were involved in intimate physical activity.' Terry explained.

'Do you know who it was?' Sharon found the courage to ask him.

'No, I don't but the gross misconduct became more serious when he tried to delete the recording.'

'Is there any camera in the filing room?' Sharon asked innocently.

'I did not know it myself; I learnt that apart from the building security with CCTV, there were some secret cameras on our floors.' Terry takes another sip from his glass while Sharon is worried hell inside. 'You see there was another camera in Doug's office which recorded his deletion, he could not deny anything. The poor man was deep in shit to his neck. I am not sure how could he get out of it and I am surprised that the matter came to light when Chuck was doing some notes on the firm's internal controls.'

Sharon felt darkness around her, she half listens and was wondering what's going to happen!

'Why couldn't he let it like that!? I am sure he would have received a severe warning from me, maybe a word of advice from Sir Henry to behave himself in future!' Terry continued.

In his enthusiasm, Terry was not able to see all kinds of colour changes on his wife, and the shock she was in. He takes another sip of the scotch; the glass was nearly empty.

'Was there any backup?' Sharon asked.

'Yes, but now all the backups have been deleted, so that there is no come back to it.'

'But surely, Doug or Gordon would have seen the girl in question?'

'I am sure they did, but they have not told me or Anwar, we had to do all the dirty work (implying firing Lenny).'

'Gordon is close to Sir Henry, no?'

'Yes he is…I am sure he would have told him but Sir Henry did not tell me either.'

Sharon is quiet for a few moments, deep in thoughts.

'You seem to be more concerned about who the girl was? He is a young bright solicitor who has probably ruined his career because he could not hold his drink…or his prick for that matter!'

Sharon is still quiet, she gets up with her empty glass and takes Terry's glass and goes to the cupboard and pours some more scotch in both glasses, and comes back giving one to Terry. She takes a big sip.

'So you will know who the girl was?' Sharon ignored his concern over Lenny's career.

'Yes, sooner or later I will know… I am sure there will be some changes in the secretarial staff.'

Sharon goes quiet again in deep thoughts. Terry who was trained to listen and interrogate people suddenly realises, 'wait a minute… I did not tell you that Lenny was in the filing room?' Suddenly, his mood changed and he snapped. Sharon knew from the very beginning that somehow or the other, Terry will know that it was she; she looks down at the floor, not able to look at him. She started crying, it does not take Terry much time to understand who was the girl!!!

It was now Terry's turn to be in shock. He could see himself as being the laughing stock of the office and all his colleagues looking at him with sympathy. So it is the department manager, the fearful Mr Terry Hamilton who could not 'hold his wife! He could never imagine Sharon doing that; she was dancing close to Chuck, he recalled while he did his PR exercise. Sharon continued to cry, she looks at Terry whose face had suddenly changed from a loving husband to a fearful lawyer. She had not seen that face many times before but knew him well. There was no point in arguing any more. 'I was that girl. Terry, I am really sorry.' Sharon admitted in low voice while her face wet with tears. Terry is lost in different world; he knew it was her before she confessed.

Terry did not like when Sharon cried which she did whenever she was upset, and this one was really too much for her. He loved her so much but he could not bear to be the laughing stock of the office. His facial expressions did not change, though the initial shock was over. 'So how long have you been screwing with him?' Terry's language had gone down the drain, in anger. Sharon in spite of being so upset, manged to lie, 'Oh it was just that evening; I think we both got drunk.'
'How can you do that to me woman?' He demanded. 'Haven't I been a good husband to you?'
'Terry, I am really sorry, it won't happen again…. ever,' she assured him.

He got up, still very angry and started walking in the lounge. Sharon is no longer crying but trying to recollect herself. Terry was thinking, how she really made a fool of him. In the party, he remembered she was dancing close to Chuck, and even at the dinner party, he did not notice them together. How very shrewd; how women deceive! The thought made him even more angry; the scotch she served did not help, his thinking getting blurred. He took the crystal glass of scotch and threw it in rage against the wall, it breaks, and some scotch left in the glass leaves its mark on the wall and the carpet. To see this violent reaction Sharon, instead of controlling herself gets annoyed, 'if you were not too busy with your PR with Pamela (Sir Henry's wife), maybe, you would be with me and I will not be in this position,' she exploded.
'Don't be fucking mad, you are not a little girl, if I do not do this PR, I would not have been where I am today.' Terry shouted.
'What about Rebecca, in the dinner party, you were falling all over her.' Sharon accused him.
'It is bloody incredible, a dance with a young woman … you are calling that falling over. I was right in front of you; you were also busy with Chris, no?' He yelled.
Sharon did not know what to say, 'whatever it is, you don't need to behave like a madman.' She shouted.
This made Terry even more angry. He rushed towards her, and slapped her hard on the face, making sure it is not too hard so as to break her teeth

which he knew he could easily have done. 'Now you have the right to call me, mad!' his voice full of sarcasm.

Sharon had never seen him so angry, this was the first time ever he had raised his hand on her. She started crying again. 'You are not any different than a very low class person who tries his strength on a woman,' tears flowing from her eyes. Terry does not reply; he sits on the chair not close to her. He realised that he had lost the edge on the argument, hitting the wife was not the right thing to do. He controls himself and looks at her still with anger.

Suddenly, Sharon gets up and comes near him, 'whatever you decide, it is up to you; but never...ever ....raise your hand on me again,' she warned him in no uncertain terms, pointing her finger close in front of his face. Before Terry could say anything, she shot off from the lounge, still crying.

That night Terry slept alone in the spare bedroom.

The same evening in an apartment in Belsize Park, Lenny is in the lounge/dining room with Joan Menzy, his girlfriend who often had dinner with him and sometimes stayed overnight. Lenny lived alone in a one bedroom apartment in a luxurious apartment block. There is a half-finished lasagne on the table and couple of glasses of red wine,

Joan realised that Lenny has been awfully quiet and lost in his own world, He hardly spoke since she arrived. He seemed to be very worried as well. 'What's the matter darling? You seem very quiet, are you alright?' She asked sympathetically.
Lenny looks at her with blank eyes, he knew there was no point hiding, 'Joan, I resigned in the office today!'

Joan is shocked; he had never mentioned any problems in the office before. 'What happened?' She asked anxiously.

'It is all office politics, they made me the scapegoat.' Lenny lied to her.

'I thought you were doing really well and that you were a rising star!'

'Yes, I was… but if something goes wrong, they have to blame someone.'

'Sorry, Lenny it is not making any sense.'

Lenny thought for a minute, how could he continue to lie, he wanted to change the subject and spend time finding another position. 'You know this guy Chris in the office, that creep has spoken against me, you see we were working on a big project together; he thinks he will do well if I was not around.' Lenny tried to convince her.

'But these kinds of things happen all the time; you do not get fired for….'

Before she could finish her sentence, Lenny interrupted, 'you see I had a row with Chris and then with Terry….without going into too much details… I decided to resign but instead of apologising or talk me out of it, the HR director accepted my resignation, apparently approved by Terry and Sir Henry.'

'Oh my God! …So it is true.' Joan was filled with grief. She gets up and walks towards him and puts her arms around him; and kisses him on his hair lightly. 'Don't worry darling, I am sure you will find even a better position soon,' she tried to console him.

Lenny is quiet, touched by her affection and puts his both hands on hers. They both leave their food unfinished and take their glasses and sit down on the sofa nearby. Joan, seeing him still quiet, goes to the radio and puts it on. The radio plays in a male voice the track 'I laugh at myself now, I don't cry' a song which seemed quite nice in the past but inappropriate in the current circumstances. Lenny got up and turned the radio off. 'Let's go somewhere else where there is some decent music and people.' Lenny said.

'I think Covent Gardens, there are some nice bars with good music, and it is always very lively.' Joan suggested.

'Great, let's do it.'

Shortly afterward, they left the flat.

Chapter 5

After the row with Sharon, next morning, Terry did not take any
breakfast at home and left for the office early. Sharon was still sleeping in
the bedroom. She noticed the main door closing after him. Terry dealt
with the commercial cases, that was his expertise but in the past, he had
been involved in some high profile divorce cases. He knew about
domestic violence which was probably the main cause of divorce, but
why the domestic violence occurred? Husband and wife misbehaving;
and not being faithful to each other. Now, he himself was involved in
domestic violence. His train continued to run fast to the City but his
mind was racing even faster. By the time, he got down from the train he
knew what he was going to do.

About an hour later, after Terry had seen all the post, emails etc, he was
in Sir Henry's office. He discussed with him that continued stay of
Lenny, since his 'resignation' was not in the firm's interest. He convinced
him to ask him to leave the same day. Sir Henry knew that it was no point
upsetting his trusted and competent head of the department, and
reluctantly agreed with him. If only he knew who was the woman? He
would not behave so cool, Sir Henry thought. He did not know that Terry
knew now who the girl in the filing room was.

Half an hour later, Terry was in Anwar's office. 'Anwar, I have seen copy of the resignation from Lenny.'

'Yes, it is right here.' Anwar handed him the original.

Terry returns the paper to him after a quick look. 'I have just been with Sir Henry; I would like you to ask Lenny to leave the office today.'

'Why so sudden?' Anwar asked ignoring that he reported to Sir Henry and not to him, and did not like the way he ordered.

'Sorry, I mean I would be obliged if you could ask him to leave today,' Terry noticing slight discomfort on Anwar's face. 'I think, his continued presence is going to cause a lot of rumours, and it is not in the interest of the morale of all the staff. And as I said Sir Henry agreed with it.'

'I see.' Anwar said.

'Chin has already taken over his role in 'Green Park International' that was the major work Lenny was handling these days.'

'It will upset him; I think we mentioned that he could leave within a few weeks, of course, well before his notice period.'

'We are going to pay him for his notice period. I will speak to Roxane (the FD of the firm) if you like.'

'Fine, but let me handle it.' Anwar decided not to argue with him. He did not like Terry's impatience.

'Thanks Anwar.' Terry gets up and leaves the office.

Anwar immediately picks up his phone and speaks to Sir Henry. Making sure that Sir Henry was in agreement with Terry; he called his secretary to dictate a letter accepting Lenny's resignation and enclosing his P45. Then he rang Roxane and explained briefly to her what had happened, and asked her to send Lenny's P45 to him.

About an hour later, Anwar entered the office of Lenny who shared it with Chin Lou. Chin was in Terry's office.

'Hi Lenny,' Anwar closed the door behind him and sat down on the chair opposite. 'I see Lou is away.'

'Yes, he is with Terry.' Lenny replied.
Anwar hands over an envelope to him which he was carrying that
contained Lenny's P45, a letter and the Exit Form. 'I am sorry this is my
unpleasant duty. That's why I came in person instead of sending it by my
secretary.'
Lenny opened the envelope and sees his P45, letter of acceptance of his
resignation and asking him to leave the same day. His face changed, sign
of unpleasantness appeared on his face. 'I thought we had agreed that I
could live within my notice period.' He complained, 'besides, it would
look so odd to leave today.'

Anwar also feels awkward, he stays quiet for a while; Lenny continued to
examine the papers.

'I would tell everyone you decided to leave today since you resigned and
I will confirm if someone asks, this way there will be no loss of face.'
Anwar sounded sympathetic.

Lenny is quiet for a few moments. 'You know I have been feeling lousy
since the morning. May be this is the best way to finish this saga.' He
takes out the company mobile phone, presses a few keys to erase
contacts, history etc and puts it on the desk in front of Anwar, and then he
moves the laptop from his side of the desk to Anwar's side and takes out
from his wallet the company credit card. He quickly completes the Exit
Form, signs it and gives the form to Anwar who also signs it and keeps it.
'Well, that's it' Lenny said in ice cool voice. 'I am sure you are doing
your duty.' he said it sarcastically while putting the envelope in his
pocket.
Anwar felt, he could not read the correct emotions on Lenny's face:
anger, sorrow, disappointment; really hard to read, maybe all.
'I know how you feel… yes I am doing my duty! You will remember my
conversation the other day; the firm will stick to it.'
'I don't give a shit about the firm now; I think the whole thing is over
blown'.
'Yes I understand your sentiments' Anwar stayed cool.

'Am I allowed to say goodbye to a few colleagues?'
'Of course, you can do that as and when you like throughout the day.'
'No, I don't think I want to be humiliated any further, I will leave right now.'
'Look, Lenny, I really am sorry but I hope you will understand the firm's position.' Anwar got up from his chair. He extended his hand. Lenny hesitated for a second then he shook his hand.

When Anwar was about to leave his office, 'do you know Mr Rampuri, the girl in the recording was Mrs Sharon Hamilton…. I think you will appreciate the scenario better now!' Lenny said it in a bitter voice. Before Anwar could reply, Lenny strode out of the office, leaving Anwar in a state of shock.

Terry got back home and found Sharon in the lounge. Normally, she will rush to the door to greet him but today she stayed in the lounge. Terry goes to the bedroom and changes his clothes and comes down to the lounge.

'Hi,' he addressed Sharon who pretended that she was reading a book. Sharon raised her head and looked at him 'Hi,' she murmured. Her eyes showing she had been upset, cried a lot, and had not slept. Terry went to the kitchen and poured some white wine from the fridge in two glasses, and came back. He offered one glass to Sharon who whispered 'thanks.' Terry sat on the chair, close to her.

'Sharon, I don't know how to start it but last night when I was in the spare room, I kept on thinking and I could not sleep for a long time….you have really let me down.'
Sharon was relieved that his voice was rather normal and not the 'ugly' voice she heard yesterday. 'I never meant to, as I said yesterday, I must

have been drunk, I apologise once again... look.' She puts her glass down on the table. 'I am not going to drink from now onward!'
Terry, who adored Sharon, and did not want to lose her at any cost, 'I am sorry too, I shouldn't have raised my hand... it is not really me. I got carried away.'

They are quiet for a few moments. Terry was thinking, is it fair to blame her? Has he not been carried away in the past? He remembered his visit last year to States where for two nights he slept with a female lawyer who worked in their Associate's offices in New York. Was he drunk? He tried to remember. No, it was just physical need, being alone and the opportunity.... a willing good looking woman!

'Terry, we have been married for many years, we have a beautiful son. You do not want to ruin a happy life just because I have been stupid one night!' Sharon mustered courage even though; she was prepared for the worst.

Terry is quiet, he does not reply. He knew he felt a little better after he managed to humiliate Lenny in the office; he did not make any effort to see Lenny, even though, he reported to him. Sharon knew it was time to press. She got up from her chair, came closer and very seductive way she put her hands around him. 'Darling I love you so much, I apologise once again.'
Terry looked into her eyes and feels she is genuinely sorry. He closes his eyes but puts his hands on her arms affectionately. Terry's mind was working fast, all arguments and counter arguments passed quickly in his mind. 'I hope we will not have this type of conversation again,' he said in a flat voice. Sharon knew that her solicitor husband was giving her a warning. She decided to deal with it another time. It was no time to waste and let the opportunity slip. She puts her hands on her breast 'no Terry, never again,' she promised.

Lenny was in his flat. Since he left the office he had been sitting in front of his laptop and had been applying for the jobs online. It did not take him much time to update his CV. He wanted to show Henry Sheldon LLP that he could find a job immediately. After a few minutes, he stops and thinks then he takes out a visiting card from his wallet and rings Raymond Baxter, senior partner of a medium sized law firm Baxter & Partners. He had met him couple of times in different meetings. Raymond Baxter's secretary replied, 'Good afternoon Baxter & Partners.'

'Can I speak to Mr Raymond Baxter, please?'

'Whom shall I say is calling him?'

'Lenny Crowe.'

'From..?'

'I was with Henry Sheldon LLP; he is a friend of mine.'

'Please hold on.'

In a moment, he heard Raymond. 'Hello Lenny, what a surprise!'

'Hi Raymond, I am looking for a job. A few weeks ago, you hinted that you had something in mind if I was interested?' Lenny decided to go straight to the point.

Raymond is quiet for a few seconds. 'Yes, I did…I am not sure if it is still available. You see one of my major clients have opened an office in Melbourne, and they were looking to employ a lawyer with some additional compliance work responsibilities.'

'I see,' Lenny is disappointed that the position was in Melbourne. He did not really want to move overseas. Raymond sensing his disappointment added, 'you see Lenny, after two years or so stint, the person will come back to the UK headquarter in London, moving up in hierarchy.'

'Could you please check if it is still available, and I will also think?'

'I will send you the details by email, if this position is still open, how quickly can you be available, depending of course if you like the post?'

'I am available immediately' replied Lenny 'I have already left Henry Sheldon.'

'What..?'

'You see I had an argument with my boss you probably know him, Terry Hamilton, and decided to resign… they agreed to let me go immediately.'

'Oh I see.' Raymond was surprised, but he knew that Lenny was very competent and bright solicitor.

'I will send you the details, I got your card.'

'Can you send it to my personal email which is
'lenny101@hotmail.com.'
'Will do; take care.'
'Thanks Raymond, bye.' Lenny put the phone down and started applying
for more jobs online.

A few hours later, Joan arrived at Lenny's apartment. They were sitting
on the sofa in the lounge. They had not eaten. Lenny was drinking a beer
and Joan had some orange juice. Lenny had not recovered from this
morning's shock in the office, he felt slightly better after he received
email that Melbourne job was still open, and it was a good position with a
good package.

'I see you still seem very worried, did you apply for the jobs?'
'Yes I did' Lenny said thinking how he should tell her. 'I was asked to
leave the office this morning; they did not want me to stay there any
longer.'
Joan is surprised, 'I thought that they had agreed to let you serve your
notice period.'
'Yes, they had but they had to humiliate me by asking to leave
immediately. This guy Chris is really a manipulating bastard.'
Joan is quiet for a few moments 'Are you sure it was not your friend but
you who was involved in that Christmas party?'
'No it has nothing to do with that.' Lenny lied again; he knew that might
mean losing his girlfriend as well as his job.
Joan does not quite believe it, but keeps quiet. 'What are you going to
do?' she asked innocently.
'Well, I have applied for a lot of jobs; I am going for an interview
tomorrow.' Lenny did not want to tell her that he job was in Australia.
'Well done, my darling, I know that you are able to deal with any
situations… let us go out for a meal, the treat is on me.'
'Yeah, it's a great idea, I need to cheer myself up and get ready for
tomorrow.'

'I will cheer you tonight; I will stay with you…how about that!'

'Great,' Lenny showed his apparent joy and enthusiasm. He wanted to be alone and have time to prepare for tomorrow.

'My only pity is that I will not be able to settle my score with Chris, I do believe that he is responsible for my humiliation.'

'You can't be sure that it is him who is responsible. Anyway, what was the argument?' Joan asked.

'Let's leave it for today.' Lenny did not want to get into it.

Shortly afterward, they left the flat.

About an hour later, they were in a restaurant in the West End. They ordered the drink and started looking at the menu. 'Shall I order for you? Joan asked.

'Yes please, I have too many things on my mind.'

Joan ordered two steak crème and a bottle of St Emillion.

'Good choice,' Lenny said. 'I forgot to tell you that this job is in Melbourne.' Lenny dropped the bombshell.

Joan was startled; she nearly dropped her drink 'Why did you not tell me?' She asked impatiently.

'Sorry … I did not think about it. Besides, my mind is not quite working normally … too many things on my mind.'

'What's going to happen to me!...are you going to travel every weekend?' She complained.

'I will work out something, the company's headquarter is in London. Besides, I will be there maximum two years.'

Joan does not reply. She knew that she was going to lose him once he goes to Australia.

'Don't worry darling, I will do something. Anyway, the job is not there yet, we don't need to count the birds in the bushes!'

Joan remained still quiet; she decided to find out what really was going on?

'I tell you what, there are some good fashion houses in Melbourne, maybe you could come with me.' Lenny did not want to lose his girlfriend as well.

'Okay, let's enjoy our dinner, once you get the job we will discuss.' Joan wanted to think as well and not make any rash decisions. In the meantime, the waiter brought the food and wine. Somehow, Joan did not enjoy the food that night.

Two days later, Meina and Joan were in a Bistro in the City. Joan knew Meina, and had met her in the office drinkups and in other parties. 'So Joan what did you want to talk about, you know it is lunch time?' Meina asked.

'Thank you for coming Meina, you know Lenny left the firm.' Joan tried to read Meina's face.

'Yes... I am really sorry, I was very surprised... he was doing so well in the office.' Meina sympathised with her.

'Do you know why Chris and Lenny had an argument?' Joan decided not to beat about the bush.

'What...? Chris did not have any argument with him; it has nothing to do with Chris.' Meina replied quickly defending her husband.

'Lenny told me that it was to do with work; they did not see eye to eye... they fought.'

Meina is quiet, she had to get back to the office; there was not much time during lunch hour, even though, she often took long lunches taking prospective candidates out or taken out by recruitment agents. 'Sorry Joan, it was Christmas party, I hope you will keep it very discrete…you are my friend, that's why I am telling you.' Meina confided.

'Oh yes….Lenny told me that one of his friends was rather drunk and misbehaved with a colleague's wife.'

'No my dear, it was Lenny himself, apparently he was caught in sexual activity in the filing room. Someone saw them and must have reported... You know Henry Sheldon LLP, they are right snooty bunch!'

Joan immediately believed Meina. She knew deep down that Lenny had been lying all along. Her facial expressions showed a lot of anger. Meina noticed change of her mood, she was sorry that she told her the truth but she had to protect her husband, it was her duty, she was sure. Joan took a big sip of the drink in front of her; she almost had tears in her eyes. Meina felt sorry for her.

'Oh my dear, don't worry, these things happen. I am sure he will find another good job, he is such a bright person ... and what a dashing personality!'

Joan knew that she had lost Lenny, he had lied, slept with other women and even did not tell her that his job was in Australia until later. She decided that she did not really love him. 'Yes he is.' Joan said in a low voice.

Meina knew that the young thing could not control Lenny, even though, she was also very beautiful.

Quietly, they started finishing their lunch.

Two days later, Lenny invited Joan to go out for dinner. To his surprise, she refused stating that she was too busy in her work, there was a shoot for the new brochure of a client company and she had to be there. After persuasion, she agreed to have a drink with him in the Centre. Lenny was surprised; normally, she would jump to any chance to go out with him. He played squash in the West End leisure centre with a friend, and not feeling bad that he had lost, he considered that after recent problems, losing a squash game was nothing. He arrived in the pub in Knightsbridge, one of his favourite spots. It was frequented by a number of celebrities living locally and sophisticated crowd. He got himself a pint of beer and waited for his girlfriend to arrive. After half an hour, he picked up the phone and rang Joan in case she had forgotten or held up in her work.

Joan arrived a few minutes later. She looked beautiful in her tight long dress and a coat. Lenny got up quickly when he saw her and kissed her lightly; he got her a rum and coke, one of her favourite drinks. 'How was your shoot? I bet you must have shown a thing or two to the young models.'

Joan looked at him and smiled, 'yes, it was my turn to raise some eyebrows.'

'Shall I order some food?' Lenny looked at the menu.

'No, I had some at the company; there was a lot of food and drinks at the shoot.'

'Do you mind if I eat something, I am starving?'

'No, please go ahead.' Joan replied.

Lenny ordered some club sandwiches for him and another drink. He did not know how to start. He was offered the job in Melbourne earlier in the afternoon and he had accepted it. Since he was available immediately, he had agreed to take it up soon. 'Joan I have accepted the job in Melbourne' he broke the news.

Joan's reaction was cool; she couldn't careless; she immediately replied, 'congratulations.'

'You are not upset? I should be leaving for Melbourne in a week or so, just after Christmas or a few days later.'

Joan is quiet for a few moments, she was thinking. 'Please don't be upset, I am going to organise a job for you over there, besides, I shall be visiting London frequently.' Lenny said.

'Oh, don't worry about me, I would be fine.' Joan grinned.

'I don't get it, I thought you were going to be upset....I can assure you I did not have much of a choice.'

'Well, you are a young man and if I may say so, quite handsome. You will find women, girls, other colleagues' wives,' Joan was full of sarcasm.

'What are you talking about?' Lenny snapped. 'Are you alright?! Did you have too much to drink at your office?'

'No Lenny, my dear, I am not drunk. You see I had a meeting the other day with Meina. I wanted to find out if Chris could work out something for you in the office.'

'You stupid woman! You were trying to work out some thing for me with Chris, that son of a bitch has caused me so much aggravation.' Lenny exploded.

'Lenny, please keep your voice down, otherwise, I will leave right away.' Joan warned him while looking around.

'Sorry darling, I did not mean to, maybe you should have discussed it with me. Meina is really a nice person but I wish I could say the same thing for her stupid husband.'

In the meantime, the waitress brought the sandwiches and drink. Lenny thanked her while she was leaving; she said, 'enjoy yourself!' Not looking at food but at Joan. Lenny managed a smile and thanked her again. Joan decided that she was tired and wanted to get back home. So she decided to come straight to the point. 'Lenny, do you know what Meina told me?…she said that it was you who was screwing a colleague's wife in the filing room,' she threw the bombshell.

Lenny is shocked, somehow he knew that that this fucking saga is going to hound him for a long time but he did not expect Joan to meet Meina. Of course, Chris could not have kept quiet, he must have opened his fucking mouth to his wife, he swore at both of them.

'Your silence and the sacking from the office prove that you are guilty!' Joan was not in a forgiving mood.

'No Joan…I promise, I did have a row with Chris, I swear, but it was not in the office...outside…you see he does not like me, he always felt threatened that I will overtake him in the office.'

'Bullshit...I don't believe you.' Joan said firmly.

'Look, I am going to explain to you more at home. Let's get back at my place, I want to really appreciate your beauty tonight,' he looked at her meaningfully.

'Sorry Lenny, I am leaving you… I had a very good time with you in the past year. You are really a smart guy but perhaps too smart for me!' she was still sarcastic.

'What are you talking about?' Lenny was amazed.

'No I mean it, I could have done it over the phone but I decided to see you last time.'

Lenny's face changed, he could not believe his ears. 'Please Joan, don't do this to me. I am already half broken, I can't bear it.' Lenny pleaded.

'I really am sorry, Lenny… you kept on lying one after the other, you take me for granted; I know a lot of people who would love to take your place,' she said in a plain voice not showing much emotions.

'Please Joan…give me another chance, I will make up to you.' Lenny begged.

'Lenny, even after all this, you took a job in Australia without consulting me. Did you really think of me? But I understand, you are an ambitious man, and you have to give your career priority.' Without waiting for his reply, Joan got up; she hardly had touched her drink. She came close to him and kissed him lightly on his cheek, 'goodbye Lenny… all the best.' She strode off the pub.

Lenny is dejected, he looked at the empty seat in front of him, then her drink, then his food; he also had not touched it. He nearly breaks down and his eyes became wet. Then he controls himself, takes out the handkerchief from his pocket, and wipes his eyes. He puts a twenty pound note on the table and leaves the pub. The waitress, seeing him leaving the pub, rushes towards the table and noticed the note, the unfinished food and drinks on the table, but before she could say thank you, Lenny had already left the pub.

It is just before Christmas, the office was basically going to close down till New Year. Even though, the office was officially opened, there was hardly anyone. Only a scant of staff and admin people attended the office between Xmas and New Year.

Terry and Sharon were invited to Chris' place in South Kensington. He lived with Meina in a two bedroom spacious apartment. The lounge/dining room was large and kitchen/breakfast room was also spacious. Chuck was leaving for New York the following day. Peter Cooper was also there with his wife Brenda.

All of them were sitting on the dining table. Sharon did not really like to come there but she did like Meina and the dinner was for Chuck. Meina was a good cook, she could prepare traditional Indian food, Italian and typical English dishes. She once confided to a friend that Chris loved her Tandoori chicken and that's why he married her!

There was mix of Indian and Chinese dishes. They were in the middle of the dinner; the glasses of Burgundy were in front of them. Chuck who was not used to Indian food, really liked Tandoori chicken, he thought it was the best he had ever eaten. Chuck looking at Meina 'you must teach me how you cook this chicken, it is really delicious.'
Meina smiled 'Thank you, I would love to do that but then the trade secrets!'
'Ah well, you can trust me, after all, I am a lawyer.' Chuck smiled back. He thought Meina was really sexy: light brown skin, medium height, dark big eyes and round hips which were quite inviting in a tight sari. Sharon noticed Chuck's appreciating looks at Meina; she knew he was from New York, and perhaps missing his girlfriend. She did not know much about him except that he was a single person, similar age as Terry.
Peter who was not much in for hot food remarked 'God… it's hot, I am going to be drunk, I keep on drinking wine.'
'Don't worry Brenda will drive, she is being very careful,' said Chris.
'You don't need to be careful, I will drop both of you on the way home, I am so used to Meina's cooking and Burgundy hardly affects me.' Terry said smilingly.
'I am quite used to French wines, thanks anyway.' Brenda smiled back.
'And I am used to French women I nearly spent six months in Paris.' Chris boasted.

'Of course, Chris could only communicate in sign language.' Meina made fun of him implying his very basic French. She could speak French reasonably fluently.

'Using sign language has got its own benefits.' Chris continued with the joke.

'Men and their boasts, all are the same.' Sharon added.

The dinner continued with light conversation and a large amount of Burgundy was consumed in the Christmas spirit. While they were having coffee after dinner, Brenda asked 'Anyone heard from Lenny?' On the mention of Lenny, a number of faces changed their colour: Terry, Sharon and Chris, even Meina was slightly uncomfortable. Suddenly, Terry remembered that he had a telephone call from Raymond Baxter asking about Lenny, and in spite of his ill feeling towards him, he gave him a good reference stating that he was really able and sharp, not stating his other 'qualities' with women. When he learnt that the job was in Australia, he had taken a sigh of relief. He only hinted that he had some personality clash with one colleague, and they were working on one project together, and before they could resolve, he decided to resign.

'God, you guys have gone so quiet!' Brenda looked at them.

'I had no problems with that guy, he did not even come to say goodbye.' Chris said it with unpleasantness on his face.

Sharon decided that it was not wise to say anything. She already had enough problems because of him. However, she thought what that guy has got, all the women fall over heels for him.

'I think he has got another job, I had a call for his reference. He is a very sharp solicitor.' Terry decided to be generous.

Sharon admired her husband, after all, he was department head and in the race to take over Sir Henry's position. Chuck smiled and an apparent reference to himself, 'some people always get what they want!'

'You mean jobs.' Brenda looked into his eyes.

'Well … that's what I meant.' Chuck chuckled.

'*Et maintenant, messieurs et mesdames, digestif pour vous?*' Meina asked.

'Come on, you don't need to show off your French,' we know you speak well.' Chris said.

'Have you got some cognac? I think it would cool those chickens in my tummy!' Peter asked.
'You need another sorbet, man.' Brenda advised.
'No… just cognac *pour moi*.' Peter also showed his French.
'I will have the same… Sharon, you are driving back?' asked Terry.
'Okay, I will drive... Meina nothing for me.' Sharon replied.
The party continued.

About three miles away in a flat Lenny was sitting depressed and drinking large quantity of scotch. He could not get over Joan leaving him. Bigger shock reduced the impact of small shocks, losing his girlfriend was definitely a big shock.

Chuck returned to New York. The project had not finished so he had to be back in the New Year. Christmas came and went and nothing remarkable happened. Everyone seemed to enjoy.

Two days after Christmas, Lenny was at Heathrow airport. He had checked in but was looking around searching for someone, he was hoping that Joan might come to say goodbye, he had sent her a text since she did not reply to his voice mail message; he had also sent a text to Sharon. After a few minutes, he decided to go to a coffee shop nearby; he had plenty of time before boarding.

'Hello Lenny,' a soft whispering voice called him.
Lenny turned back it was not Joan but Sharon. For a few seconds he was disappointed, he was really hoping to see Joan. 'Hi Sharon... what a pleasant surprise! You did not reply to the text.'

Sharon does not reply but comes closer and kisses him on his both cheeks with affection, looked more like a sister or casual friend kissing, rather than a lover. 'Shall we go to the café?' Sharon asked. They walked into the café and ordered coffees.

'Lenny I was shocked when I heard that you resigned, and so suddenly decided to leave the office and the country as well, you never informed me.' Sharon complained.

'I did not want to cause you any harm, I know you wanted to keep away from me… I believe it was the right thing to do.' Lenny said it sadly.

'Oh I wish I could come with you Lenny, I missed you so much.'

'Please don't make it more difficult than it is already, you don't want to ruin your life.'

'I did not tell you, Terry knows everything. I had to confess when he said that soon he will know who the girl was?'

'I am sure apart from Chris, a number of people know in the office. However, I do not think it is a common knowledge. Gordon and Doug must have known if they saw the recording, even though, I had deleted.'

'I don't know and I don't care, if Terry knows that's all I cared… I nearly lost him.' Sharon said thoughtfully. 'But let me not bore you with mine; why did you decide to leave the country, you could have found a job in London?'

'It is a good job with a good package and after two years, I can come back to London and work in the headquarters, so I managed to save my career to a certain degree.' Lenny looked sad.

'But why are you looking so sad? Have you not been sleeping well… wait a minute…Where is Joan?' Sharon suddenly remembered his girlfriend.

Lenny took a sip from the coffee. He is quiet and his eyes are almost wet.

'She left me,' he said almost in tears.

'What….. I thought she was so much in love with you!'

Lenny looks at Sharon in her eyes, 'you never know who is in love with whom? If she loved me enough, she wouldn't have left me.'

'Oh my poor darling,' Sharon puts her arms around him with affection. 'But who told her about the office?'

'That our 'friend' Mr Chris Sneale!!!'

Sharon is surprised and her facial expressions show she had just swallowed some bitter pills. 'Did she know him?'

'No, apparently Chris told Meina that I left the company and the reasons for it. Joan met Meina.'

'Did she mention me?' Sharon asked quickly.

'No… Meina and Joan do not know who was the girl, so this secret is safe to a certain degree…Do you know Sharon they humiliated me in the office, they asked me to leave the office the same day!' Lenny's face was full of grief.

'You should have told me all this before... maybe, I could have done something.' Sharon felt really sorry for him.

'No, you couldn't have. I am glad that you and Terry are okay… I guess Sir Henry and Anwar must have given a good reference, otherwise, I wouldn't even have got this job.' Lenny groaned.

'Terry is very intelligent person, and he really loves me that is why we are still together... it was Terry who gave a good reference for you!' Lenny couldn't believe. 'I know he is very sharp, he is really going to go high up...but I am fucked. My job is gone, my girlfriend is gone, my peace of mind is gone, I really feel that I am being thrown out of the country… just because Chris could not be a colleague for a minute, and keep quiet.'

'Yes, I know.' Sharon went into deep thoughts.

'He could have just ignored. After all, it was Christmas, lots of people had fun.' Lenny put all the blame on Chris.

Sharon is also sad and full of hatred for Chris 'One day, I will settle the score with Chris, my darling you look after yourself.' Sharon said it with a firm resolution. Then she looked at her watch.

'No there is still enough time.' Lenny wanted to spend some more time with her. For a minute, he thought I wish Sharon was coming with him. But Sharon was far above his reach. 'I did not expect to see you at the airport. I thought you would call me.' Lenny tried to control his emotions.

'No I wanted to see you; I was shocked to learn that you were leaving the country... I really love you,' her eyes full of love and sadness, a tear almost dropping from it... They both got up from the sofa where they were sitting; he took his briefcase.

Near the departure gate, Lenny hugged Sharon tight, and then kissed her on the lips, 'Goodbye Sharon; I really appreciate you coming here.' Sharon looked at him and then put her lips again on his...a long passionate kiss.

Two people at the airport not quite knowing who did they really love. Their long kiss was interrupted by an announcement about the flight to Melbourne. 'Goodbye my darling and bon voyage.' Sharon managed to say while Lenny rushed to the departure gate.

Far in the corner at the departure gate, a woman dressed in a long coat with dark glasses and a cap which almost hid her face, and who had been observing carefully Lenny and Sharon, started crying... she could not even say 'goodbye'.

Chapter 6

Almost three weeks passed. New year came and went, lot of well to do solicitors came back after visiting Bali, St Lucia and other exotic places. Henry Sheldon LLP got busy as usual. Chuck was also back from New York; he had briefed Sandy Gorfield about his UK trip and the progress he had made in his secret due diligence of the firm. He also visited briefly Langley, and made a brief report to his superior officer. The report confirmed his earlier findings that 'Xany' (a code name for one of the suspects under investigation) had bought the property through an offshore company in which Xany was neither a shareholder nor officer. However, the nominee directors' secret records confirmed that he owned the company. He had checked all the information in the files of Henry Sheldon LLP.

One after noon, there was a presentation in the board room of Henry Sheldon; Roxane was doing the presentation. Sir Henry, Terry, Simon Randall (the other head of the property business), compliance manger, Anwar and the management accountant were there. It was the preliminary financial review of the year end results. On the wall, there was a giant screen which could show from Bloomberg to TV and acted as screen for the presentation. There was a laptop connected to the screen and Roxane had a laser pointer in her hand. On the screen, there was management Profit & Loss account. 'The gross fees have gone up by about 62% which was above the budgeted figure of 53%. The reason for increase was (she presses the button, and it opened another window which showed the breakdown of the fees by department). There was a 75% increase in the

commercial work, couple of investigations for FCA and some major advisory work on an acquisition.' She stops and picks up her glass of water. ... 'I am sure Terry can explain more,' she looked at Terry.
'Well, we had two PLC clients added during the year, a number of projects started last year, some of them continued this year, and produced more chargeable hours than we had anticipated.' Terry said proudly.
Sir Henry smiled, looked pleased what he had seen. 'Well, it has been a real good team work last year,' he remarked.
Roxane continued; moved on to various costs and its analyses to finally on the bottom line. Everyone looked and raised questions; they were all very interested in the year's results. For solicitors, their interest in the financial figures seemed commendable. 'Well, this is the most important number, the net profit for the year, it has gone up by a massive 55%.' Roxane proudly presented the figures.
'Why the net profit is lower in percentage term than the gross fees?' Anwar asked.
'This is because we have had some one off expenses. Firstly, the modernisation of the office which has not been capitalised, then major expenditure on new server, some new laptops, one off some new security devices and some payroll cost... I could go in more details if you like.' Roxane asked.
'No that's fine, I got a good idea.' Anwar was pleased he asked the question; others seem to be as interested in it.

The meeting continued and after a few more slides, 'I would like to point out that these are provisional figures subject to audit.' Roxane sat down. 'I am sure with your expertise, the audited numbers will not be any different.' Sir Henry praised his financial director. 'Thank you dear,' he added.

Everyone clapped slightly, and the meeting was over.

Next day, there was a meeting in Terry's office. Chuck, Chris, Peter and Chin were sitting there.

'I am really excited; Hashim Al-Zor could really strengthen "Green Park International".' Terry said.

'I think Green Park will have a good entry in the Middle Eastern markets with their co-operation.' Chuck remarked.

'I had a meeting with the CFO of Green Park International, and he was asking if we could appraise this guy up. Is he really serious or just want to know about the company's business? Terry pointed out.

'But why can't they do it themselves?' Chris asked.

'May be because they do not wish to give things away, they think that we will be more discrete. Besides, they do not wish to have their staff too much involved with Hashim…I think they are a little sceptical about his visit.' Peter explained.

'Chuck, why don't you take him out... or wait.. take Chin or Peter with you.' Terry suggested.

'I think Chris will be the right person since he knows the company really well and London too.' Chuck said.

'I know the guy, I met him before very briefly; he wanted to take some interest in Tower International.' Chris said.

Terry thinks for a few moments. 'Well it is settled then, Chris and Peter will take him out after the meeting. Chris I let you co-ordinate it.'

Chris was happy for a good opportunity. He was thinking if Terry had known his part in the Christmas party saga and Lenny, he would not be so nice with him. 'I will be delighted,' he replied.

After a few minutes, the meeting was over.

Near Bond Street in the heart of Mayfair, is an exclusive hotel frequented by businessmen, celebrities, and head of states. It is evening and the restaurant is nearly full, waiters in smart uniforms have been serving quality food at quality prices to people not too worried about the prices.

At a table of four, three men in smart business suits are sitting. These are Chris Sneale, Peter Cooper and Hashim Al-Zor. Hashim is from an important Middle Eastern state. He is in his late twenties, dressed in a smart business suit. He has a light brown complexion and wears a moustache. He is from a wealthy family and acts like CEO of his family business called House of Al-Zor. They have nearly finished their main course; a waiter comes and refills their glasses. They thank him. They have been discussing "Green Park International". Hashim takes a sip of his wine 'this is really good Bordeaux; these guys know their wine,' he praised the quality of the wine.

'It is really to do with your choice; I spent a bit of time in Paris and learnt a little about wines.' Chris tried to show off since he chose the wine.

'I see you are a real connoisseur, my compliments to your good taste.' Hashim praised him.

'Thank you, I am not a connoisseur but one does acquire a little knowledge living in the country.'

Chris looks at an enquiring face towards Hashim. 'No thanks, not for me, I am fine,' he said in a flawless English accent showing his Oxford education.

'Not for me either, but perhaps some cheese.' Peter said.

Chris looks at the waiter. 'Can we have the cheeseboard here and then we can select.'

'Very well sir', the waiter replied obediently and walks away.

'I hope you don't mind me saying so, but your English accent is really good.' Peter praised Hashim's English.

'Oh, it's nothing, since last twenty years or so, a lot of my countrymen study in Europe and in the USA, I studied in Oxford.'

'I see.' Peter said.

'Okay, let's talk about Green Park International, I learnt quite a lot this morning in the meeting in their office... we are really looking for an interest that company, say about ten to fifteen percent, that is the real reason for my visit.' Hashim changed the subject.

'We had some idea but not the extent of your interest... have you done your due diligence?' Chris asked.

'Not really, I had Companies House searches, a report from our accountants' associates from here… but frankly we invest in people as much as in their business.' Hashim takes another sip from his glass. 'We know they have some excellent people working for them.'

Peter was impressed, 'they have been our client for a long time; in fact, the majority shareholder has been our client for decades.' Chris was happy the way the conversation was going.

'I am sure we will be able to assist you in reaching a satisfactory agreement.' Peter remarked.

'Yes, I am sure you will.' Hashim looked at both of them in their eyes. Chris and Peter did not quite get it that it was just a matter of optimism or something more to it. In the meantime, the waiter served them the cheese from the cheeseboard and conversation drifted to English cheese versus French cheese.

About an hour later, after a round of coffee, they left the restaurant. Chris and Peter left the hotel while Hashim went to his room; he was staying in the hotel.

Sharon and Terry were watching TV in the lounge of their home and drinking coffee in the evening. There was news about China buying fewer metals from Australia affecting the worldwide collapse in the metal market. Sharon remembered Lenny. He had never called her since he left for Australia. She did not have his new telephone number; she dared not asking Terry about his new company. Suddenly, her facial expressions changed, she remembered how miserable he looked at the airport; how the poor man was so dejected. He lost a lot and what was the reason? She could not blame her indiscretion, after all a lot of women do, Christmas is definitely a time for celebration. She knew a lot of other women who had done worst. It was that rascal Chris. She felt like taking the crystal vase nearby and breaking it over his head.

'What's the matter with you darling...are you alright?' Terry asked with genuine concern in his voice.

'Sorry, what do you mean?' Sharon did not realise that Terry had noticed
her facial expressions. 'Oh, I was thinking about a colleague of mine in
the gallery.'
'You were not planning to send a drone to him or her!' Terry smiled.
'No darling, we women are a little more subtle, we don't attack people
like men!' Sharon forced a laugh.
'Well as long as I am in your good books!'
'You will know when we are in bed!!' Sharon looked at him in the eyes.

Two days later, Chris, Chuck, Peter and Hashim are having a drink in a
club in Mayfair. The club was well known, the idea was to mix the
business with pleasure. They have been discussing "Green Park
International" earlier at the company's offices. All of them had cocktail
glasses in front.

'It is really nice over here.' Chuck remarked, seeing all kind of smart
people and very well dressed ladies, he recognised one well known
Hollywood actress.
'Yes, it is one of the best.' Chris who was a member of the club, said
proudly.
Peter who had not been to this club before was also impressed. 'I think I
would like to become a member as well.'
Hashim who had been to all kind of clubs not only in London but also all
over Europe just smiled. 'These guys really know what they are doing,
did you see their forecast?' Hashim wanted to make the best out of his
visit to London.
Peter knew immediately that he was referring to Green Park
International,'and would you believe those were the conservative
numbers!'
'I think we are going to get somewhere, my dad is going to be happy.'
Hashim smiled.
'If the price is right, I guess!' Chuck said, 'one does not need to get
carried away.'

Chris did not like Chuck's remark but he hid his displeasure. He decided not to bring Chuck in the future PR exercise.

They continued to discuss. About couple of hours later, they left the club. Chris and Peter shared a taxi while Hashim took another one to his hotel. Chuck decided that he wanted to have a bit of fresh air so he walked in the street. The night was quiet; the streets were the same, occasionally, a car passed by. Chris turned into a side street suddenly and waited. A moment later, a man turned into the same street. Chuck immediately caught the man with a surprise, and the man bent down with pain when Chuck suddenly landed a punch into his tummy. Chuck helped him straighten up but holding him in such a way that he could not retaliate. The man had some of his ribs broken. 'Why were you following me?' Chuck demanded in an aggressive voice.
'I was… I was… just going to the tube station,' the man could not speak properly due to pain.
'I noticed you in the club; you have been watching us the whole evening. Tell me who are you? You… son of a bitch.' Chuck gave him another punch in his tummy. The man realised that Chuck was far too stronger. He had not fallen; he quickly put his hand in his pocket to search for something. Chuck immediately held his hand and put his other hand in the man's pocket. There was a small canister of chemical inside. He took it out and threw it a few yards away. Then holding the man, he looked at his other pocket and took out some papers. After looking, he knew immediately that he was not from British secret service. 'I am not an Arab, you son of a bitch. Next time before following, make sure who the people are!' Chuck put heavy American accent. The man decided not to retaliate. He realised that that was a punch from some professional with black belt, maybe a high ranking dan. Besides, two punches had already caused him enough damage. Chuck took a listening device from the man's pocket and put it in his own pocket. 'If I see you anywhere near me again, I will make sure that you and your boss will never walk in a street on your legs.' Chuck warned him in an ice cold voice. He also took out his phone and took the man's photo before letting him loose. The

relieved man left quickly, not looking back, holding his tummy with one hand. Chuck waited for him to turn into another street. Then he went into the opposite direction, and caught a taxi for his hotel.

Two days later, Chris, Meina and Hashim were in a restaurant in Marylebone area. This area has many nice restaurants, and is one of the gourmet centres of the capital. Meina was in a nice mid length skirt and both men were in business suit. They were just shown to their table which Chris had reserved. Hashim was quite impressed by Meina, if he did not know that she was Indian origin, she could be mistaken for a girl from his own country. They were drinking their aperitif after ordering the food.

'Please tell me about yourself, I mistook you as a lady from my own country.' Hashim asked.

'Very simple really, I was born in London but my parents came from Delhi, a long time ago. They are originally from Pakistan…moved to India during partition… I work in the HR department of Russell Appleby, chartered accountants, in the City.' Meina tried to sound modest.

'Yes I know them; they are an international firm. Hashim said, 'You know I met some Indian and Pakistani girls in the university, they were all very intelligent.'

'Only intelligent?' Meina teased.

'I mean… they were all very intelligent and some of them were really beautiful.'

'So how come you do not have an Indian wife?' Chris asked.

'I do not wish to be bound by family responsibilities at young age. I did date a couple of girls casually…. You see I want to make really big, my family is rich but I want to take my family business to twenty first century.' Hashim could not hide his ambition.

'So you want to be a 'shogun' in business!' Meina smiled.

'Not quite!'

The waiter brought the starter and they got busy in it while continuing talking. While they were having their main course, Hashim remarked that the food was excellent.

'It is a cordon bleu restaurant, quite well known among the business circle.' Chris said.

'Sorry Meina... I mean Mrs Sneale... can I call you Meina?' Hashim was not sure if he could call her by her first name.

'Please do call me Meina; I am not really as old as I look.' Meina replied.

'Oh no, you look very young.... and if I may say so, very beautiful.' Hashim complimented.

'You see, we solicitors do our due diligence even on our women before choosing them.' Chris grinned.

They all laugh. 'You certainly do!' Hashim thought she really looked sexy.

'On the subject of due diligence, sorry to change the subject... what do you think of Alan's presentation?' Chris asked.

Hashim thought for a moment' I believe the indicative price is too high... but let's leave the business for a while and talk about your beautiful lady.'

'There is really very little to talk about me... tell us, have you got a girlfriend?' Meina asked as though she knew him for some time.

'Yes, I do have a girlfriend; she is studying in the university back at home.' Hashim sounded happy talking about his girlfriend.

'Maybe in your next visit, you can bring her with you and stay with us.' Chris proposed.

'Perhaps, if she has her mid-term break; but in our society, women do not stay with a man prior to getting married.' Hashim replied thoughtfully. Suddenly, he started missing Aliya. 'But maybe you both could visit us some time; my family would be honoured to receive you.'

'That would be nice, something to think about.' Chris said.

Hashim opened his briefcase and took out a bag containing a large bottle of 'Chanel' perfume. He offered it to Chris, 'May I offer this small gift for your wife.'

'Oh, you shouldn't.' Chris said quickly.

'No please, I would be very pleased.'

Chris thought for a few moments, he knew to refuse it, will offend Hashim. 'Then give it to Meina yourself,' and looked at her, suggesting her to accept it.

Hashim moved the bag in his hands towards Meina 'I will be honoured if you accept it.'

Meina looked at Chris then took the bag, and took out the bottle from it. 'I am delighted; this is my favourite perfume; thank you very much.'

'My pleasure, madame.' Hashim was very humble.

Meina admired his false modesty. They continued with their dinner and occasionally talk. Meina thought Hashim was really a wonderful man.

It was weekend. Meina and Chris were visiting Meina's family. They lived in Wimbledon, a middle class suburb of London. Meina's father had died a few years ago; his mum lived with her elder brother Balak Kapoor. Balak managed two chemist shops, originally started by his late father. He is in his early thirties; a few years ago his engagement was broken, since the fiancé from New Delhi married someone else locally. He never found the right girl since then.

They were all sitting in the lounge which was tastefully decorated.

'Mumiji, can we eat early, Chris has to go to a business meeting?' Meina asked her mum, Leena.

'Yes sure, but what is this meeting on Saturday night?' Leena asked.

'Mumiji, a client of ours is visiting London and he is going to return soon, I have to discuss some office business with him.' Chris explained.

'You guys, instead of making children, too busy in work ....thou shalt rest on weekends!' Balak looked at his sister meaningfully.

'We want to have children after you... aren't you my elder brother?' Meina smiled mischievously.

'Well, you have to find your bhabi (sister-in-law) first, before I could do that.' Balak said.

'I do not want grandchildren without marriage… that's sure.' Leena added.

'I know just the right girl for you; a colleague of mine left the country recently, leaving his girlfriend behind.' Chris said.

'Who is this girl you are hiding from me?' Meina complained to her husband. Before Chris could reply she remembered, 'of course, you are talking about Joan.'

'Let me know when you arrange a date for me with her.' Balak went along with the joke.

'Sure, Meina knows her well, she can organise it very quickly.' Chris said.

'I will think about it.' Meina did not sound very enthusiastic…. 'The poor girl, she was almost in tears when Lenny was fired.'

Chris thought about Lenny and Sharon but did not say anything.

They moved to the dining table which was on the other side of the big lounge.

About an hour later, Chris left Wimbledon.

Near Green Park, there is a famous casino. It is very popular and is considered to be one of the best casinos in London, frequented by businessmen and non-businessmen alike. Chris parked his car nearby in the street and walked towards the casino where two security guards in their fine uniforms were standing. They looked at him closely but let him pass considering that he looked a responsible person. At the gate, there was a beautiful glamorous girl, dressed in a smart mid-length skirt who welcomed him.

The receptionist did not recognise him and asked. 'Good evening Sir, are you a member?'

'Good evening, no I am not a member but I am supposed to meet a friend of mine, Mr Hashim Al-Zor.'

'Oh, Mr Al-Zor, of course. Could you please wait a second,' she pressed a number on her phone and speaks to someone. 'He will be with you in a minute, if you would like to wait over there,' she said politely and leads him to the sofa nearby.

'Thanks.' Chris sat down.

Soon Hashim came, 'good evening Chris.' Hashim extended his hand. Chris shook his hand and they both walked to the main hall of the casino.

Chris had been to casinos a few times but he was not a gambler. He was quite impressed with the atmosphere in this casino. Smartly dressed men and women of various ages, some sitting, some drinking and other playing on the roulette tables, blackjack tables and others. Most of the croupiers were girls with their shapely bodies and very tight dresses, busy entertaining their customers and making money for the casino. Hashim noticed his appreciative looks for the croupiers; he knew the man lusts after women. 'Shall we get some drinks?' Hashim asked him. 'Yeah sure.' And they walked towards the bar.

About half an hour later, Chris and Hashim were on the roulette table. Hashim had taken five thousand pounds chips paying in cash. Chris asked him, 'how come you carry such large amounts in cash?'

'I come from a cash society, and carrying large sums of cash is not unusual for us. Besides, I do not want my family to know my gambling habits. I am not a habitual gambler but to go to casinos for relaxation.'

'I see.' Chris couldn't quite work out how come he was a member of the club; did he visit London so often?

Hashim put five hundred pounds worth of chips on the black colour and won. After couple of more rounds, where he put the money on certain numbers and colours, he handed a large number of chips worth several thousand pounds to Chris. 'It's your turn now...let's multiply.'

Chris was reluctant. 'No, please …I have really no experience.'

'Don't worry Chris, most of it is winning… even if you lose it, it's not a big deal!' Hashim encouraged him.

Chris did not really want to play but since it was winning from the casino anyway, he decided to try his luck. He played on the colours and was really excited when he won twice. 'You see, you know about roulette more than I do.' Hashim remarked.

'It's beginners' luck! I am sure.' Chris tried to play it down. Then he tried on certain numbers and lost some chips.

Hashim and Chris enjoyed the evening at casino without giving any regard to how much money they were winning or losing. About an hour later, they retired to the luxurious chairs and ordered some drinks. They still had a lot of chips in their hands.

'Sorry to change the subject, do you know why Alan is insisting on such a high price?' Hashim asked.

'Sorry Hashim, the drinks and excitement at the casino table and my mind measuring the vital statistics of the croupiers, it is not easy… but I think Alan did point out the future prospects. They have really a strong balance sheet.' Chris tried to explain.

'Future prospects are in the bush … yes I admit the balance sheet is strong, even though, there are some large loans… but still the question remains…. and their P&L does not justify the multiple they are asking for.' Hashim complained.

About a minute passed, while Chris tried to concentrate, he knew the real reasons why they were insisting at higher price but did not wish to disclose. It will be compromising the firm and his work in Green Park International 'I am not an accountant; perhaps, you need to check with your advisers.'

Hashim was disappointed with the reply but he hides it. 'Yeah, sure… let's got back to the table.'

They got up with their drinks and chips, and go back to the roulette table. They played; won a few times and lost quite a few bets. About an hour later, Chris realised that he did not have any chips left. 'Sorry but my luck seems to have run out, all my chips have gone.' Chris said disappointingly.

'No worries, take mine.' Hashim handed over his remaining chips to Chris.

'No thanks, I have already lost you a lot of money.'

'But I insist, these were mostly winning, so there is not a real loss… besides, with roulette you never know!'

A few minutes later, they both were sitting at the chairs near the bar. Chris was not happy, having lost all the chips he had. 'Don't worry Chris, it is nothing… I won't tell you how much I lost once in one night over here!' Hashim tried to console him.

Chris looked at him, 'don't tell me you lost more than five thousand in one night!'

Hashim laughed. 'A lot more, my friend... a lot more. I know people who have lost close to one million over here, in one night!!'

Chris was shocked who has got so much money to burn, he thought; we solicitors are a lot more responsible people. 'You guys have money to burn, if I had lost five thousand pounds in one night, it would take me weeks to recover.'

Hashim is quiet for a few moments. He did not want to tell him that they had nearly twenty thousand pounds worth of chips between them, 'let's call it a day.'

They both finished their drinks.

The weekend passed. On Monday morning, Roxane is in Sir Henry's office.

'Roxane, you wanted to see me?' asked Sir Henry.

'Yes sir,' she opened a file containing expense claim forms for Chris Sneale. 'Sir, Chris has been claiming lavish entertaining expenses, Terry has approved these but I wanted to check with you.'

'Let me have a look.' Sir Henry asked her.

Roxane gave him the file; he looked at the claim forms briefly, and handed it back to her. 'How are you treating these in the books?'
'Subject to your approval, I was planning to put them under the Clients Entertaining.' Roxane replied.
'No, we need to recharge all these to Green Park International… you see Chris has been working on a special project, the clients had requested to look after this new investor.'
'I see.' Roxane replied.
'If you see Terry, he would fill you in… ..I am having regular briefs on this project from him. Terry thinks Chris is doing a great job.'
'Thank you Sir, I will see him...I will also ask him if we can recharge some additional hours for Chris?'
Sir Henry smiled. 'Sure, you do that.'

Roxane got up and left Sir Henry happy in his office.

Chapter 7

In Mill Hill, North London, there is a pub, quite impressive, a detached Tudor style building with real log fire place, Mahogany furniture, and typical English pub decoration. At one table, Sharon, Terry and Chris are sitting. Chuck and Terry are drinking Real English Ale and Sharon some cognac. Terry had invited Chuck to the pub after dinner at their home. Chuck wanted to see a real English pub and this was a traditional English pub. They had been there for a while, their glasses were almost empty.

Chuck looks at his watch. 'I should get going.'
Terry looked at his watch, 'it is only six thirty in New York; the night is still very young!'
'Sure, it is time for the happy hour over there.' Chuck smiled.
'Why not have another one?' Sharon asked.
'Okay, I can't refuse a lady... Let's have another one and then I must hit home.'
Terry got up and walked to the bar.
Sharon looks at Chuck in eyes, 'Chuck I need your help.'
Chuck is surprised. 'Yes mam…..what can I do for you?'
Sharon looks around, everyone nearby was lost in their drinks and/or conversation. 'You remember Lenny, the guy who was fired recently.' Sharon whispered.
'Yeah, I do; the guy who went to Australia?' Chuck pretended he had no knowledge except what was said officially in the office.
'Do you know why he was fired?' Sharon asked.

'I think he got a better offer from Australia... they must have offered him a good package... gold cufflinks as it is known in the industry...he was doing rather well in the company.'

'I was responsible for him leaving. You see, I am the guilty person.'

'I don't understand mam... Why should you think so?' Chuck pretended to be real surprised.

'I do not think so; it is the fact.' Sharon's voice showed real sadness. Chuck is quiet, he knew it very well but he did not want to embarrass her. 'You see Chuck,' Sharon used her charm and spoke to him with confidence like she knew him for a long time and they were close friends. 'I happened to be very stupid at the last office Christmas party...,' before she could complete the sentence, she noticed Terry coming back with two glasses, she stopped. Chuck also looked in that direction.

Soon Terry was there. 'Sorry darling, the barmaid is bringing your drink,' he said while giving one glass to Chuck who thanked him. In a few moments, barmaid brought the drink for Sharon.

They raised their glasses and said 'cheers' simultaneously. 'To your visit to London.' Terry added.

'Thanks Terry.' Chuck appreciated.

After a few minutes, Terry excused himself; he needed to go to the toilet. Sharon looked at him and once he was away, she said, 'someone saw Lenny and me that night.... and the whole saga started from there,' she hesitated but did not go into details about Lenny deleting the CCTV footage.

Chuck acts as though he was shocked. 'Did that person spill the beans?' Chuck asked innocently.

'No, but the whole thing got messy when Lenny realised that someone had seen us, after all, I am the wife of his boss.'

Chuck really did not want to get into details; he knew everything except who was the person who saw them but he did not care. Lenny was gone; it did not make any difference now. 'Are you being blackmailed?'

'No, but that person caused lot of damage to me... you see Terry learnt it.' Sharon confessed.

'I see…..no wonder he was asked to leave the same day after his resignation.' Chuck recalled.

'It has caused me a lot of pain and… and I feel I need to settle my score with that person.' Sharon's voice sounded like whisper.

Chuck was amazed, women! He thought why can't they let bygone be bygone? 'Who was the person who saw you?' Chuck suddenly showed a lot more interest.

'It was Chris', she muttered biting her lip.

Chuck was genuinely surprised. 'Does Terry know that as well?' Chuck knew that Terry was really appreciative of Chris work in Green Park International.

'No, Terry does not know that.' Sharon replied.

'How can I help you mam…?'

'I want him also to be fired!' Sharon said it with a firm resolution.

Sharon noticed Terry was coming back, she quickly adds 'I will speak to you over the phone another time, but I think you got the idea', she looks at him into his eyes. 'I will reward you suitably!'

Later that night, Chuck is in his bedroom at the hotel where he was staying. He kept on thinking about what Sharon had told him. How come he did not recognise Chris in the CCTV recording? Then he thought of Lenny. Did Chris really blackmail Sharon or she just wanted to take revenge on someone to satisfy her? What help could he give to her! He was wondering. Suddenly, his mobile rang and he looked at it. Immediately, he knew it was Langley. He entered the code. 'Sorry Zero, can I call you in a few seconds?' Cuck said, and before the other side could reply he terminated the call. He immediately left the room and went to the bar area at the ground floor. After buying Bourbon, he went to the hotel lawn where there was hardly any person, few empty chairs and tables. Chuck looked around carefully and sat down in corner table facing the door of the bar. He takes a small sip of the drink and dials on his mobile and calls Zero.

'Hi.' Zero replied.

'You called me?' asked Chuck.

'Yes, I was summoned by 'Big Daddy' (director), he received a complaint against you.'

'Sorry, what complaint!?' Chuck was surprised.

'You have been bashing up a friendly services' agent.' Zero's voice was serious.

'That guy was pestering me; following me and was recording my conversation with some office colleagues.' Chuck raised his voice.

'Well, these 'Mazeltoves' have contacts at the highest level here… you need to stay low; do you follow?' Zero ignored his complaint.

'Yes, I do, but… .' Before Chuck could finish his sentence, Zero interrupted, 'you don't work for us officially, we will have to deny everything, you understand?'

'Yes, I do.' Chuck was not happy.

'You see, you left us officially about five years ago, and that is the official version.'

'I know but it seems you guys are scared of them.'

'No, we are not.' Zero replied emphatically. 'That guy was carrying a gun, he could…'

'He wasn't, I searched him.' Chuck cut his sentence.

'It does not matter now…. I think it is enough…Anyway, is Hashim clean?' Zero asked.

'Yes, he is… he wants to be the Buffett of Middle East!'

'Good.'

'I was going to ring you about Mega Ponzi (reference to a major US scam); I believe some of the funds have been channelled through 'Green Park International' to various countries with final destination to a Middle Eastern country.'

'Maybe that's why you were being followed…Look… do you need any help?' Zero sounded enthusiastic.

'Perhaps…… I will let you know.'

'Can we trace these? I am sure IRS and Fed will be very interested.' Zero's seemed pleased with the new discovery.

'I will see if I can get more info on it.......fine, I will be in touch.'
'You would remember what I said to you earlier.' Zero advised him to be careful again.
'Yes...bye.' Chuck disconnected the phone.

Next night, after dinner, Chris is in his flat after coming back from the office. He was examining some office papers after dinner. Meina was watching TV, his phone rang, the other side, it was Hashim.
'Can we meet for a short period, if you are not too busy?' Hashim asked.
'Well, I was looking at some of the reports... I have a meeting tomorrow morning.'
'It shouldn't take very long.'
'Couldn't we discuss it over the phone?' Chris asked.
'Sorry, no. I need to discuss something important with you.' Hashim replied. 'You see I will be shortly going back …. to discuss the deal with my family.'
'Alright, I will be at your hotel in ten-fifteen minutes.'
'Thanks, Chris.' Hashim seemed happy with his reply. Meina who has been listening to their conversation worked out that he was going somewhere, 'who is it darling? Your office never leaves you in peace even at nights!' She complained.
'It is not the office….it was Hashim, he needs to discuss something.'
'Aren't you seeing him too much, don't you see him in the office?'
'It is a very important deal for our client, and of course, really big one for us! Terry is happy with the progress and Sir Henry too, I understand.'
'That's alright but you only met him on Saturday, and spent hours with him!'
Chris gets up and put his papers back in the briefcase. He comes close to Meina and kisses her on her head. 'Oh, my darling…you don't understand, this is an opportunity of the life time to make my mark. I won't be long. I promise to make you happy later!' Chris said it in a charming way.

Meina understood what he meant, 'promises!! .. I know I will be fast asleep by the time you come back.'
'No, I will be back shortly.' Chris went to the bedroom to put his leather jacket on.

About an hour later, Chris and Hashim are sitting in the hotel lounge with coffees in front of them. They have been discussing the business.
'Chris if you would like to work for us, it will be a great help.' Hashim proposed.
'Hashim, how can I work for you when I am working for Henry Sheldon LLP, and in turn for Green Park International?' Chris could not believe that Hashim will make such a suggestion.
'Perhaps, I have not explained very well. I am not suggesting that you leave your current job, what I am saying is that you work for us as well.'
'But that will be almost impossible...conflict of interest, client trust and all kinds of issues… sorry Hashim this does not make any sense.'
'You see Chris, no one needs to know that you are also working for us; basically, we will use your expertise and advice to negotiate a better deal for us' Hashim tried to convince him.
Chris realised that work ethics and practices were still very different in his country. 'Hashim, this will not work. I cannot work for two employers. It will affect my fiduciary duty with the client and clearly will be a conflict of interest.'
'You do not need to tell anyone about it! It will be an arrangement between us, not even written. We can pay 50% of your time in advance and 50% on completion of the deal.' Hashim could not really see any major problems.
Chris looked at him, and is quiet for a few moments. When Hashim noticed his face, 'and let me say we will pay it offshore or in any jurisdiction of your choice, even to the numbered Swiss bank account,' he whispered bringing his face close to him.

'I am sorry Hashim, it is not practical… it will be considered proceeds of crime and will have exposure to Money Laundering Act, we both could be in deep shit!'

'Look… where I come from, these kinds of arrangements are not unusual. You are providing expertise and we pay for it!'

Chris takes a sip of the coffee. Hashim immediately orders some more fresh coffee for both of them. Chris was thinking how can he refuse him politely or maybe, he should take a chance. Hashim does not push him; they both are quiet for a while. 'What kind of money we are talking about?' Chris finally asked.

'Look Chris, I am a fair person, I know one has to pay for expertise… Alan is insisting on such a high price… if with your skill and help, we can save a bit of money, then a five percent of savings or let me be generous… ten percent of savings.'

'I don't understand.'

'Let me clarify to you. You see a fifteen percent stake in Green Park is about forty five millions, if we can get it say for thirty five millions, we are saving ten millions…ten percent of ten million is a cool one million!'

'Oh God, it's so tempting' Chris looked around. It was getting late, and there were only a very few people in the lounge, no one was sitting close who could over-hear them.

The waiter brought more coffee. Chris took a big sip of fresh coffee, it tasted good. Hashim knew that Chris was getting tempted. 'Chris this is probably a good opportunity for you, we are not asking you to do anything wrong, we are merely seeking your expertise with perfectly legal transaction and willing to pay for it.'

Chris listened carefully what Hashim said, he excused himself and goes to the toilet. He put some cold water on his face. He just wanted a little more time to think straight. He considered the risks and the large sum of money. I could buy two flats in London and rent it out or maybe, buy a holiday home in Spain. It would be really nice, he thought. He made a decision and walked back.

Hashim smiled when Chris sat down. 'You seem a bit more relaxed now, maybe, I should also go to the toilet!!' He joked.

'I am a solicitor; I don't make rash decisions.' Chris said. 'I am interested in your proposal but I will meet with you tomorrow to confirm it.'

Hashim is quiet for a few seconds, his brain also working very fast; he knew he was almost there. 'No problem, I will see you tomorrow. I understand these kinds of decisions are not discussed over the phone!'

Chris felt relieved that Hashim did not press for the decision there and then, I could always change my mind, he thought.

About an hour later, Chris is in bed with Meina in his flat. Meina noticed that he was restless. 'What's the matter, darling? You seem a bit restless.' Chris could not tell her all kinds of thoughts in his mind.

'You should have taken some cognac, it always helps... do you want me to fetch it for you?'

'No, I have been drinking too much since last few days ... too much alcohol is not good for me, tomorrow a number of meetings.' Chris was pleased that she cared.

'In that case, let me cuddle you, she turned towards his side and puts her hands on his shoulder and brings her face close to him. He kissed her but the kiss does not last longer. Meina is quiet, and tries to sleep but senses that Chris is really very tense. 'You can't sleep, can you?' She asked.

'I have got too many things on my mind.' Chris replied.

'It is time to switch off darling...otherwise you will get old before time!' she looked at him meaningfully.

'I can't sleep.' Chris complained.

'I know exactly what you need!' she lifted his shirt and put her mouth on his tummy then she worked South.

Chris could not believe, 'I thought you didn't like it!?'

'I know but I want to be a good wife, it's time to be in twenty first century...my Indian blood cannot allow me not to please my husband!'

Chris smiled. Meina worked hard to please him. Chris thought it must be his day; first it was the good deal from Hashim, and now Meina finally, getting to be like a normal wife… he continued to think the beautiful house close to the beach. He put his hand on her hair. Meina showed real expertise on something she did not like! It wasn't long before Chris climaxed, and shortly afterwards, he fell asleep. Meina is disappointed, all that work for nothing in return. 'Men are really selfish bastards,' she thought. However, she felt a little satisfaction that she had been a good Indian wife whose duty was to please her husband. She turned from side to side for a few minutes, she could not sleep. Luckily, she also knew how to release her tension! After a few minutes, she also fell asleep.

Next day, Chris could not concentrate on anything in the office. He just wanted to come back home early. While he was attending the meetings or working in the office, his mind was in the forthcoming meeting with Hashim.

That day was too long for Chris.

It was late in the evening; Chris rushed to Hashim's hotel after a quick dinner with his wife Meina. She played an understanding wife who knew her husband's business commitment were important for his career.

Chris and Hashim are in the sitting in the hotel lounge more or less the same places where they were night before. A bottle of Champagne is in front of them in the ice bucket, and the flute glasses are half full still with some bubbles in it. They had discussed briefly the position. Hashim raised his glass, 'let me welcome you to House of Al-Zor.'
Chris also raised his glass. 'Cheers.'

'Let's get down to serious business now.' Chris said.
'Okay… what is on your mind?' asked Hashim.

Chris discretely looked around, no one was sitting close by; everyone seemed to be interested in their own business. 'I am willing to provide you my services but obviously it has to be absolutely confidential… you should not even disclose it to anyone except perhaps to your father.'
'Agreed.' Hashim said in a matter of fact voice.
'We cannot have anything in writing, so there has to be mutual trust.'
'Yeah, sure.'
'This is my account overseas in Euro; I use it for various reasons particularly, for holidays. I would like you to transfer the advance you suggested yesterday into this account.' Chris gave him a piece of paper with the account's details.

Hashim looked at the paper, thought for a short while. 'Even though, we would like to buy Bank of England we do not keep much funds in liquid. These kinds of payments come from a special account, but I can only do it in small amounts.'
'What do you mean?'
'I mean if you had agreed yesterday, I would have got the necessary okay from my family…they know what I am planning.'
'Alright then… we can meet tomorrow.' Chris was disappointed.
Hashim was thinking. 'Look,' he takes out his mobile I can transfer one hundred thousand pounds to your account straight away; the balance of advance will take couple of days…or maybe tomorrow. As you said we have to trust each other.'
Chris said, 'fine, I have absolute trust in you.'

Hashim pressed a few keys in his mobile and transfer hundred thousand pounds. 'Well, it is done.' Hashim extends his hand to shake. Chris shakes his hand and they both pick up their glasses. 'Cheers,' they both said.

Shortly afterward, there was a ring on Hashim's mobile, he speaks to the person. The bank had required his verbal confirmation 'Yes, that's fine.' Hashim said on the phone and terminates the short conversation.
'Congratulations, the funds are in your account.' Hashim said. 'You can check it in your account.'
Chris wanted to check but he decided it was not a good idea; he needs to show his confidence. 'Thank you, your words are good enough for me.'

They both reflect what they had done for a while.

'Hashim, I am going to tell you a plan whereby you can probably pay even less than thirty five millions.'
'I am all ears.' Hashim smiled.
'You see, Green Park International is under investigation by FCA. We are helping them; we are also closely involved in their other business deals... The company has some gold mining interest in Africa, due to the recent price slumps in the metal market including gold; the banks are not very keen to finance it. So they need the money. It is a good deal apparently because cost of production is still quite low compared to the gold price. But it will take a while to turn that gold into sterling. Are you with me?'
'Yes, I understand, please continue.' Hashim was as sharp, his eyes sparkled with interest.
'In addition, the company has got plans to go for IPO which you know about, but there is a company which is very interested in acquiring them but they prefer IPO, and could do with financing; your cash would come very handy.' Chris took a sip from his glass. 'They can have adequate financing without bank's time consuming agreements etc. You know how tight the banks are at the moment, in spite of low interest rates!'
Hashim looks at Chris with more interest.
'With your finance and with more or less certain success in the gold project, they will go IPO with higher valuation, so you see!'
'I understand absolutely... Without our funds, they risk delaying their gold project and probably not realising the true potential in their IPO.'
Chris looked at Hashim; he could not believe Hashim will understand the position so quickly, his eyes showed admiration for Hashim. Age is not

the key to the business acumen, he thought. 'There are some other points, I will explain as we go along.'

They continued to talk the finer details. In the luxurious hotel's lounge, two happy men continued with their discussion till late.

When Chris returned home, he went to his laptop and checked his online bank account. He was glad to see a large sum in his account. Hashim is an honest man, he thought.

Meina was waiting for him. 'You look very happy today,' she remarked.

'Today, I am a lot more relaxed.' Chris took her into his arms and kissed her.

'Can we wait till we are in the bed?'

'Of course, my lady… whatever you say.'

That night Meina did not have to do anything. It was Chris's turn to make her happy and he did it with his hands, mouth and……

Chapter 8

Next day, Chris was in the office, he could not concentrate much because his mind was always on this 'new project'. He already planned in his mind how he was going to deal with it but he knew that he had to be very careful, in case someone notices that he was working for two masters or he was caught in breaching the fiduciary duty he owed to his office and Green Park International. He did some company searches; spoke to the banks and Green Park International's external accountants. He knew the price of his indiscretion would be his professional life. FCA were getting all very efficient, he thought, Law Society had also very sharp teeth; they were so concerned about solicitors' image and standing in the public!

In the afternoon, he had a meeting with Alan Davis the CFO of Green Park and his financial controller, Mark Beale and the CEO Wolfgang Helmut (Wolfie). Peter Cooper, Chuck Orcel and Chin Lou were also in the meeting. They have been discussing FCA investigation and then the conversation came on House of Al-Zor.

'I heard you are really getting along well with Hashim.' Wolfie looked at Chris.
'Yes, I have had a number of meetings with him along with Peter and Chuck. 'I also met Hashim socially and have given my input to Alan.'
'Good, Alan told me that he is very interested but there seems to be some issues with the pricing.' Wolfie looked at Alan.
'Yes, that is correct; he is looking about 30% lower.' Alan looked at Mark who nodded.

'I think we need to explain to him very clearly the planned IPO or even the interest of another company.' Peter explained.

'No, I don't think we want to get any third parties involved, if he contacts them it may not be a good idea,' Alan said, 'besides IPO is a better option.'

'Perhaps, the gold project needs to be spelled out.' Chuck gave his opinion.

'No, he knows we have some gold interest but I do not wish to give him detailed information, in case, he walks away with it.' Alan showed his reservation.

'I agree.' Wolfie said. 'Gentlemen, if you will excuse me, I have to attend another meeting; you need to work out the right way to extract the highest possible price; Alan please see me after the meeting.' Wolfie got up and left the board room.

'Mark is going to do a brief presentation on the latest result... I just wish to add that even though, the results are good, expenditure on Gold Project has affected the cashflow, and the bankers are not at all keen to extend additional facility without premium rate and even then, it is not sure.' Alan laid down the position.

'Let's look at the numbers.' Chris looked at Mark who got up and went near the screen. Mark presented the management accounts and then there was a discussion, everyone participated. It seemed that everyone was well prepared. Chris definitely was!!!

In the evening, Chris and Meina were getting ready to go for a meal with Balak Kapoor and his new girlfriend Irena Makowski, an East European girl who was working as marketing manager in an Italian food importer. While Meina was in the bathroom, Chris took out his spare phone which was not registered under his name; he used to ring the people he wanted to keep confidential. He rang Hashim and explained to him the main points of the meeting in the office. Hashim was pleased that his intended

purchase was discussed seriously and that the price was becoming more negotiable. Hashim asked Chris. 'Shall we meet for a short while?'
'Sorry can't make today, I am going out with Meina. It is her brother and it is important.'
'Of course... the family always comes first.' Hashim was quiet for a few moments. 'By the way I spoke to my dad and I am transferring another one hundred fifty thousand to your account then two hundred fifty thousand will be on agreement and the balance on completion.'
'I trust you.' Chris replied, wondering how come people trust so much, if the deal falls through and I don't pay him back, it is really very little they can do. 'You got my bank details.'
'Yes, I have... give my regards to your family.' Hashim said; 'I am going back and will be back in a few days.'
'Yes, Alan said the final meeting with you is next week.'
'That's right, I need to consult my family and come back with a firm plan, now the matter seems to be progressing.'
'I will look after your interest Hashim; I will continue to work in this project. Shortly, there will be a major meeting and I think your proposed interest will be the main topic.'
'You are an intelligent man, I am sure you will know how to deal with it. I shall be meeting our UK adviser about shareholders' agreement clauses.'
'That's great, have a nice trip, if I don't speak to you before you go back.'
'See you Chris...and thanks for your help.'
'My pleasure, see you.' Chris pressed his mobile to terminate the conversation.

Couple of days passed. Chris continued with the project work and Green Park International; he continued to influence Alan that they should reduce their valuation and that it would be better for IPO that some important overseas business would have an interest in the company. Peter Cooper noticed the shift in Chris's position; he thought Chris was very eager to get the deal through. He knew that he was very ambitious, and success in the deal would be a definite plus for his career within Henry Sheldon LLP. In spite of his concern, he did not point it to Terry.

Terry and Sir Henry were away for couple of days to Brussels for business. They had to have meetings with the clients whose head office was over there. Sharon took advantage of being alone; her son was in boarding school. She arranged to meet Chuck for dinner in the Centre.

In the evening, they were sitting in a fashionable restaurant close to Bond Street, the very chic street of London. Sharon was looking very beautiful; a fashionable dress and good make up she looked also very elegant. Chuck was impressed; she looked a lot younger and sexy. But then it was the night to impress. Chuck was dressed in a smart evening suit as well. They were looking at the menu, 'what would you like Chuck?' Sharon asked.

'You ... mam.... Sorry, I meant you decide.'

'Can you just call me Sharon; it sounds too formal 'mam?'

'From the young age, my mum told me to address all the ladies as mam... she said, it had its own advantages apart from being polite!!!'

'We will talk about advantages later; but tonight just Sharon,' her smile was too charming.

'Alright...Sharon.' Chuck smiled back.

'Tonight you are my guest, so you decide what would you like to have?' Sharon knew what he had meant when he said 'you' but it was too early to have that kind of conversation; there was the whole night.

'Well, I am a steak man, perhaps "*steak au poivre*" with salad and some potatoes.'

'No starter.'

'No, I will skip it.'

'What about wine?'

'I leave it to you; I think red will be fine with steak but I am equally happy with white.'

'Fine.'

Sharon ordered the food and the wine to the waiter.

After a few moments quietness, 'so shoot, you wanted to discuss
something.' Chuck looked at her appreciating her beauty.
'I just wanted to spend some time with you. Since Terry was away, I
thought it was a good opportunity.'
'Great, I would rather spend time with you than these serious human
beings (referring to the solicitors).'
'Thank you, I take it as a compliment. I hope you will not find the wife of
a solicitor boring.'
'No ... Sharon I am delighted to be with you.'

In the meantime, the waiter brought the wine and also some fresh rolls
with butter. He poured a small quantity of wine in the glass in front of
Chuck, he tasted it 'That's fine,' and the waiter served the wine to Sharon
and Chuck; and went away.
Sharon took a sip of wine; 'do you have a girlfriend Chuck?'
'Yes and no, I know a number of women but not a steady girlfriend….
You see I was divorced a few years ago but since then I never met the
right woman.'
'I see… you mean someone like me!' Sharon joked.
'I would have jumped at the opportunity, Sharon!' Chuck said seriously.
'Even though, you know about my indiscretion with Lenny!'
'We all make mistakes; after all, to err is human.'
'As long as we do not err too often!' Sharon looked into his eyes.

Chuck was not sure how to read her statement, he decided to stay quiet.
In the meantime, the waiter brought the food, they started eating. They
continued to talk and eat. From time to time, Chuck looked around
discretely.
'What's the matter, are you looking for someone?' Sharon noticed his
eyes wandering often around.
'It's nothing, my apologies for bad manners, it is my old habit.'

Sharon knew he was looking to see if someone familiar was around or too interested in their conversation. 'This is a very nice restaurant, frequented by businessmen and polished people, no one is really interested what others are doing or talking.'
'I am sure it is, as I said, it is one of my bad habits.'
'What other bad habits have you got Chuck?' Sharon teased him.
'That is the only one, the rest are all good.' Chuck smiled.
'We will see!'

After finishing the main course, they had some cheese with grapes.
'Would you like some digestif, they serve excellent vintage port here.' Sharon asked.
'Are you having some?' Chuck asked.
'No, I am driving, can't really.'
'In that case, let's have some coffee.'

At coffee, Sharon decided to discuss the main reason for her meeting with him. 'Chuck you remember what I said to you the other day in the pub?'
'Yes, I do, you never did call me to explain it further.'
'You see, I did not want to discuss it on telephone; these days, you never know who else is listening!'
'I see…Mrs James Bond…!' Chuck joked.
'No seriously,' Sharon said, 'I need to get Chris fired …the same way as he got Lenny fired.'
Chuck wondered if she was in love with Lenny or it was just to get even.
'What would you like me to do Sharon?' Chuck asked gently.
'See if you can find something on him, I am getting to know his wife better, but she is so faithful to him!'
'Well, Chris is really doing well in the office, Terry is really impressed by him, and I am sure Sir Henry too; I am also sure he has a got a good career ahead of him in the firm.'
'He is very ambitious, a bit greedy and lusts after all the women, I am sure you must have noticed it in the office.'
'Not really, I am too busy in my work… I have to go back to New York for a few days, then I will be back to finish off my project.'

'Do you like London? Why don't you get yourself transferred here? I can introduce you to some nice girls, like Meina, Joan and others.'

'I do like London, maybe one day, I will move here but I could always meet good women anywhere.'

'Chuck, you need to think some way, I could still remember Lenny, the poor man literally got his life upside down. Joan is also unhappy because she could not forget him and has not yet met anybody she likes.'

'Alright I will put my mind to it... you said that there was going to be some reward...what did you have in mind?' Chuck looked into her eyes mischievously.

'I will invite you to meet Joan, she is really a very nice girl, you will also get a real friend in me...you know, Terry is probably going to be future Sir Henry, so it should come very handy!'

'Sharon, I was joking, I do not need any rewards. You and Terry have really been so nice with me, I would like to help if I could... you need to tell me all about his background, his finances if you know, his affairs including with you, anything to go by.'

'No, I never had any affair with him. I always have declined his advances in the past.' Sharon said it quickly. Then she explained whatever she knew about Chris, but really there was not very much.

They continued to talk for a while then Sharon looked at her watch. 'It is getting late, tomorrow is the office.'

'Okay. Let's go' Chuck agreed.

Sharon insisted paying the bill claiming that it is she who had invited him. When they got out of the restaurant, they walked towards where Sharon's car was parked. 'Shall I drop you at your hotel on my way?' Sharon asked.

'Are you sure.... I can take a taxi.'

'No, it's no problem, I am still sobers.'

They got into Sharon's car.

About an hour later, Sharon was having some Bourbon with Chuck in his room. Chuck was sitting next to her on the sofa. 'This is really potent,' Sharon remarked, 'my head is turning.'

'This is men's drink... lady! You should have stayed with Gin or Vodka!'

'Oh yes … I can hold my drink.' Sharon boasted.

'Sure you can.' Chuck poured some more in her glass. 'Cheers, to your health,' he raised his glass. Sharon had no choice but to drink some more. Finally, she felt a strong man sitting next to him! She was surprised that he did not make any move... Lenny would have been to the 'second round' by now!! She thought. The warm room with warmer spirit inside her, and a strong man next to her and the privacy of the room, alone…one did not need many reasons to take the matter further. Chuck also realised that it was right time to make the next move. He put his hand on her tummy. 'God, I can feel the Bourbon!' Sharon looked at him, he looked so similar to Lenny at the moment, she did not move but let him feel her tummy. She brought her mouth close to him, Chuuk did not waste any time; he immediately started kissing her. In a few moments, Chuck's hand seemed to slip from her tummy to her pants. Sharon could feel his warm body, his lips on hers, and now the weight of a strong hand on her pants. It did not take long before Chuck's finger slipped inside her pants. Sharon did not like to play hard, especially, when the offer was too tempting! She thought for a few moments. 'Is there a bloody camera in this room? She whispered.

'Don't worry, there is none; they don't put cameras in the guests' bedrooms. There is no Chris either on this side of the room. Come and have a look for yourself,' he takes her hand, and pulls her gently towards the bed. 'See, no one is here!'

Sharon did not need to reply, she did not even look around; there was no time to waste. She intentionally bent in front of him, 'let me look underneath!' Chuck could not resist the opportunity, he grabbed her bottom. Soon both of them were naked in the bed. Chuck noticed that she was even more beautiful with her clothes off than her clothes on. He could not wait to get inside her. His hands did not take much time before she was pulling him towards him. 'God, you are beautiful!' he whispered as he entered in her.

Sharon did not reply; she wanted him to make her scream just like Lenny used to do, and she was not disappointed. What he lacked in the looks compared to Lenny, he more than made up in his expertise, strong body and very very strong fingers!!

About an hour later, Sharon and Chuck were still in bed. 'Would you like some more drink?' Chuck asked.
'No just a little water.'
Chuck got up; Sharon saw him first time completely naked, a six foot muscular man who seemed very fit. She looked from top to bottom, she noticed two big scars on his back; one looked like a cut of knife and another a round wound. Chuck brought her some mineral water bottle from the fridge, 'sorry can't find another glass.'
'That's fine; she took a big sip from the bottle. 'I don't think I am able to drive, maybe, I will call a taxi home.' Sharon asked.
'You do not have to go home. Terry wouldn't be back until tomorrow night?'
'But I should go home, it is late.'
Chuck immediately put his lips on hers and one hand on her breast, 'I think I need to have a three course meal now, I let it go in the restaurant!!'
Sharon did not reply, it wasn't long before Chuck was on his second course. Of course, for the dessert, he had to wait till the third round.

Sharon, very tired, very satisfied, left early in the morning.

In the morning at the office, Chuck was tired, he hardly slept during the night and 'worked' very hard with Sharon. It was long time since anyone made him work so hard! He tried to concentrate in his work but could not. He kept on thinking what a beautiful woman Sharon was, everything about her was just exquisite; he could understand why Terry would not let her go, even after knowing her indiscretion with Lenny. Somehow, he thought, she was not quite unfamiliar with those situations; there must have been a few 'Lennys' in her life. He was trying to work out how to return the favour to her. Has he agreed to do anything….? Not really, but the meal and the courtesies in the bedroom had obliged him to do something about it. Then there could be a few more passionate nights with Sharon!!

Late in the afternoon, Chuck went to Gordon Moore's office. Gordon was about to leave for the day, a number of staff had already left.

'Hi Gordon.' Chuck said in a friendly manner.

'Good evening Chuck, how are you doing?' Gordon smiled.

'I am making a very good progress in Green Park International project and also doing a few other things for Sir Henry.'

'Good…. I don't see you very often; perhaps, we can go for a real Scotch one evening ... I know just the place not far.' Gordon although sceptical about him, did like him. Chuck looked to him as one of his soldiers rather than a lawyer.

'That would be nice; I am leaving for New York tomorrow… but I will be back, in a few days' time; perhaps then if you are free.' Chuck replied.

'Sure, it would be my pleasure.'

'I just wanted to ask you if Anwar gave you some papers, I noticed; he and his secretary have both left for the day.'

'No, he did not ...what papers are these?' Gordon showed his surprise. For him discipline and timeliness was so important.

'It is to do with the LLP's organisation chart, reporting lines, brief responsibilities etc. I gave him to review and then get your sign off too.'

'Do you want me to call him?' Gordon asked, and moved his hand on the telephone.

'No please, no… it can wait till tomorrow. I will be here in the morning…. Perhaps, I can show those papers to you for your approval.'

Gordon felt important. 'Of course, I will be here first thing in the morning.'

'Thank you Gordon, I am glad I stopped by. Maybe I will just pass by through his desk to see if he left them there.' Before Gordon could say anything, Chuck added, 'I would love to try some real scotch... I want to see how real Scotch compares with our Bourbon!'

Gordon forgot what they were talking about. 'Sure you will find that for real Scotch, there is really no substitute,' he said proudly.

'Let me not hold you...see you tomorrow.'

'Good night, Chuck.'

Chuck left Gordon's office and came back to his office. He noticed a number of people leaving for the day. He wanted to wait a little more. He was thinking what a nice office, people so friendly, everyone seemed to be interested in their work, if his office bought this practice, perhaps, he could be the UK boss. Sandy liked him, and had full confidence in him but Terry was heir apparent... I wonder if he will agree to him being the boss. He started looking at some papers but he was finding it difficult to concentrate. Every now and then, he could remember the beautiful body of Sharon; she is a wonderful woman, what it would be like to have her every day!!

About an hour later, Chuck was in Anwar's office. He pretended to look at his desk for a while, and then suddenly, he moved towards the locked cabinet where personnel files were kept. He pulled the drawer but it was locked. He took out the keyring from his pocket and tried one of the special keys he had. The drawer's lock clicked immediately. Chuck looked around; he knew that there was no CCTV in that room. He quickly went through the alphabetic files and took out Chris Sneale's personnel file. He quickly turned pages, saw his annual appraisal which showed he was doing really well in the firm; he turned pages to see if he could find anything ... no luck, it was just a normal ambitious competent professional's file. Finally, he was about to put it back, then he wrote on a piece of paper Chris's bank details where monthly paycheck was sent. Very gently, he put the file back making sure nothing looked disturbed in

the drawer or in the file. Then he locked the drawer. After making sure
that no one was close by, he went back to his office.

The same evening, Chris, after dinner, was working in the lounge on his
laptop. Meina was also on the other side of the lounge, watching TV. He
checked his overseas bank account online and noticed that one hundred
fifty thousand sterling had been deposited in his account. He had quarter
of a million pounds plus some of his own savings. It made him really
happy. Hashim was back to Gulf, to consult his family. He thought what
it is like to be able to make decisions just like that, and be able to play
with large sums of money. He was impressed with Hashim, smart guy, he
is definitely going somewhere! The dream to buy a holiday home in
Spain looked real, without having to wait for years or promotion in the
office.

Chris had been working hard on the project and was close to convincing
Alan and his colleagues that it was in their best interest to make the deal
with Hashim, and that the bankers were averse to the risk in the current
environment. Alan knew well the position, he also had realised that
House of Al-Zor will be very beneficial for them, a reputable Middle
Eastern company. However, he was surprised that they were insisting to
bring the prices a lot lower. Chris' enthusiasm, he read it as his eagerness
to see the project completed, he knew that Chris was very ambitious.
Next week was the big meeting which he, Terry and Hashim were
attending at Green Park International office. That will absolutely decide
the fate if he was going to get a place in Spain or will have to refund the
money to Hashim.

Finally, the big day arrived. There was a meeting in the boardroom of Henry Sheldon LLP. Terry, Chris, Peter, Chuck and Chin were in from the solicitors working with Green Park International who were also in force: Wolfie the CEO, Alan the CFO and his FC Mark. Hashim Al-Zor was there with his financial adviser and his lawyer.

After the introduction by Terry, Wolfie did the presentation showing the prospects of Green Park International, its diversified interests and the imminent IPO towards making the company a significant player in financial services sector. Alan summarised the financial position of the company, a strong balance sheet but ignoring the fact that they were practically turned down by the banks for their continuation of gold mining project and the slump of the gold prices.

Then it was Hashim Al-Zor's turn who gave brief background information about House of Al-Zor. What position they held in their country and some of the interests they already held in the UK and the USA. He pointed out strongly that his proposed interest acquisition was for long term. He finished by saying that it was in the interest of both companies for them to have an interest in Green Park International. After that, it was his financial adviser who gave a summarised balance sheet of House of Al-Zor. The significant funds they had at their disposal and how a stake in Green Park will work for both of them. Also, the fact, that they could introduce a number of high net worth clients to Green Park International.

There was a general discussion; everyone was in favour of House of Al-Zor acquiring an interest in Green Park. The only problem was the price. Terry, Alan and House of Al-Zor's financial adviser Jeremy Reynold and Chris argued about the price. There were some mini presentations by Chuck and Mark supporting Green Park's valuation, while Jeremy argued for the case of House of Al-Zor. The discussion was long and detailed. Fresh coffee was served.

Then Chris did a small presentation showing the tangible benefits of association between the two companies. Although in the immediate past, he had almost agreed the price suggested by Al-Zor but today he proposed a compromise to get the matter move forward. Suddenly, Sir Henry entered the Board room. Wolfie who was sitting at the Chairman' seat wanted to move but Sir Henry stopped him, and sat on an empty seat. The meeting continued. The discussion was still heated, both sides arguing about the price.

Finally, Sir Henry got up and pointed out how great Green Park International had the prospects, and that an association with Al-Zor would enhance those prospects. He also pointed out to Hashim that their company was acquiring the interest at pre IPO prices and they had a lot to gain as well. And that a few millions should not stop on something which will bring in tens or even hundreds of millions in the future.

The words from senior professional do help and there was an agreement. The price agreed was thirty eight millions. Hashim and Wolfie shook hands. The financial and legal experts were to draw the necessary documents.

Everyone was happy, the meeting had been successful. Alan was pleased that they managed to get an extra three million while Hashim though that they had saved seven millions. Chris was overjoyed; he did not require a financial expert to calculate that ten percent of seven million was seven hundred thousand, close to nine hundred thousand Euros. He wasn't far short of one million he had planned. Terry was also pleased; he could see a huge bill for his firm's services and strengthening his own position.

Some shrewd businessmen with their equally sharp advisers continued to discuss the matter, all with much more smiles now.

Later that evening, Chris wanted to meet Hashim but he was too busy and was taken out by Alan Davis and few others from Green Park. But late at night, he received a call from Hashim. He and Meina were in their bedroom, both were reading books. Chris took his mobile to the lounge so that he could speak freely. He did not wish to share his 'arrangement' with Meina as yet.

'How was your dinner?' asked Chris.
'It was great, I am surprised Alan did not invite you guys… he said that he planned to do a big reception once the deal was signed.' Hashim was tired so he stopped. The whole day negotiation and then the dinner with people he did not know very well.
'Perhaps we can meet tomorrow?' proposed Chris.
'Sorry Chris, I am planning to take the draft agreement tomorrow to discuss it with my family.'
'When will you be back?'
'In a few days.' Hashim replied. 'But I want to say that you have been magnificent in your argument and negotiation, and I believe that we have saved seven millions.'
'I wish I could do more.'
'No my friend… you have done an excellent job…I am grateful to you…my family is going to be really pleased.' Hashim was enthusiastic in his praise.
'Thank you Hashim.' Chris was pleased.
'By the way, our arrangement remains as agreed. I am going to transfer another hundred thousand tonight and the balance of fifty percent which is another three hundred fifty thousand, on the completion of the deal' Hashim said. 'Are you happy with it?'
'More than happy… you really are a great person.'
'The talent and the favour need to be rewarded, that is my philosophy… thank you for your efforts.'
'Thank you Hashim, I really appreciate it.'
'I will see you on my return.'
'Sure, I am looking forward to it' Chris was eager to show his appreciation.

'Bye Chris.'
'Bye Hashim.'

Chapter 9

Three weeks passed. During this time House of Al-Zor became a significant shareholder of Green Park International, the deal went through and ratified by both companies' board of directors. The funds transferred and Hashim al-Zor was a non-executive director of Green Park International, as part of the deal. There was a big party and a number of people from Green Park International, Henry Sheldon LLP and advisers were invited in an exclusive restaurant of an exclusive hotel in Strand. Hashim Al-Zor also attended the party, came over especially for it from Gulf. Chris had also received the balance of three hundred fifty thousand pounds from Hashim. Chuck went back to New York; his other work in Green Park was slightly delayed due to Al-Zor deal.

At the weekend, Chris and Meina were visiting Majorca, a beautiful island in Spain. They had been there before. The island was very popular with British people and the British influence was apparent in many quarters of island. English retirees living there, English pubs, restaurant, estate agents and shops, they were all there.

Meina and Chris were in swimming costume and had been swimming in the sunny weather. For the time of the year, it was still reasonably warm but they did not stay long in the water. They went to nearby beach restaurant and ordered some drinks. They had been reasonably quiet enjoying the weather and swim. Finally, Chris broke the silence 'you know Meina, I have been thinking about buying a small holiday house here.'

'That would be really lovely; it really is a beautiful place.' Meina was delighted to hear.

'You look very pretty in this island; you mix up well with all the Spanish beauties around!'

'I know this place has certain effect on you, you become more Italian with wonderful lies... I bet soon you will say that you will love me for a thousand year!!'

'No, I will say I will love you for ever.' Chris smiled. 'But seriously, what do you think?'

'Are you getting banker's bonus this year as opposed to a lawyer's!!'

'Something like that,' Chris thought for a moment, 'you see I have struck gold!'

'Really!' Meina's mouth opened slightly in amazement.

'You know I have been working on the Green Park project. Hashim asked me to do some work for him and I have been paid well for my services.' Chris looked around to make sure that no one was listening to their conversation.

'God... you never mentioned that before, you keep secret from your wife who loves you so much!!'

'No, it is just that things happened so fast and the payment was dependent upon the successful outcome, I did not wish to raise false hopes.'

'I see.' Meina came closer and kissed her husband. 'So can we really afford a house or a small apartment?'

'I have got close one million Euros sitting in my bank account... I think we can afford a good house with swimming pool.'

Meina took a big sip from her drink. She was happy that her husband was not only a solicitor but also a good businessman. Perhaps, they could start a family soon.

'Hey... where are you?' Chris asked, seeing her in deep thoughts.

'I was thinking, maybe we can start a family soon.'

'All in good time, let's deal with it first... tell me first about the place here?'

'I already said, it will be really lovely, my darling.'

'So drink up, we have to meet a couple of estate agents who will show us a few properties.'

'How come….? I have a feeling that you have been planning this thing for a while!'
'Not really, I just looked through some properties last week on internet and set up meetings with a few estate agents.'
Meina is pleased. 'Well done. You deserve a reward for this planning,' she brought her mouth a little forward to kiss him.
'Can we wait till the evening, tonight, I am going to play a reluctant husband!! ?'
'You can play whatever you like… man; you are going to be punished for hiding things from your loving wife!' Meina played with him.
'Okay, I look forward to that; let's finish the drinks, we have a lot to do.'

The young couple, in Spanish sunshine, glowed happiness and love, finished their drinks quickly.

Carlos, the waiter was disappointed seeing them leaving, he fancied Meina.

On Monday morning Chris was in the office as usual. He was still involved in Green Park International project. He needed to check with Terry something. In spite of ringing him and his secretary a few times, he could not contact him. He was tied up according to his secretary.

While Chris was being restless in his office, in Jersey International Bank, the day is as usual. St Helier's financial district is busy with moving money, assets and keeping up with all the exciting news of international banks particularly, in Britain and the USA. One of the trainee accounts managers, Anthony who was examining his portfolio of clients, noticed unusual movement in one of the accounts. He went to see his boss, the accounts manager for personal customers. 'Jacques, this is what I wanted to see you about,' said Anthony showing a print out to him.
Jacques looked at the printout; it is not very material; most of our customers have large balances.'

'But if you look at the past movements, the balances were in thousands.'
'Let me have a look' said Jacques, he typed in some keys in his computer; his eyes widened 'yes, you are right; the past transactions were relatively low value.'
'Shall I block this account?' asked Anthony.
'No, just because these are comparatively large balances it does not mean that these are not genuine. I think we need to bring it to the attention of Compliance Department.'
'Shall I do that?' Anthony was enthusiastic MBA who joined the bank about a year ago.
'No, I will look into it a little more, and then will inform Compliance Department with your suspicions and my comments.'
Anthony got up.
'I like your diligence Anthony. I will copy you on the email. Money Laundering Officer may want to talk to you.'
'That's fine; thank you.' Anthony started moving.
'Discretion is important, right?'
'Yes Sir, I understand.' Anthony left Jacque's office.

Tuesday morning, Henry Sheldon LLP's office has got a rather sombre look. There is a meeting in Terry's office with a very serious agenda this time. Only Terry, Anwar and Chris are there. Terry is in his chair behind the desk; Anwar and Chris are sitting in front of him. Terry has got a computer paper labelled 'Strictly Confidential' on the desk. Terry explained to Chris that there was a report that Chris had been working with Hashim Al-Zor to influence the lower price on the Green Park International deal, and that he was accused of taking bribes from him. Chris is startled. He could not believe his ears; until last week he was commended for his efforts to close the deal, today, he was accused of malpractice, breaking the fiduciary relationship with client. 'On what basis you can say that?' Chris almost shouted, trying to get out of the situation.

'Look Chris, you are an intelligent and responsible lawyer, we would not accuse you unless we had some very serious basis and support for it.... and please keep your voice low.' Terry's voice was full of disappointment and showed a little anger.

'Terry, how can you accuse me of such horrendous things?' Chris knew that no one could disclose the arrangement he had with Hashim.

'Alright than, explain how come you have nearly a million Euros sitting in your offshore bank account?' Terry looked straight into his eyes.

Chris knew the game was up. In spite of him not having emails or piece of paper about that account, somehow, the information leaked. 'I do not understand, having funds in my personal account which I am not saying I have, has anything to do with the office.' Chris raised his voice again.

'We will not be having this meeting unless we had substantial proof... are you denying that you do not have these funds?' Anwar said in a cool voice.

Chris is quiet for a minute, he was not prepared for it but he was an experienced lawyer. His sharp brain helped him, 'I have got some funds belonging to a friend to buy a property for him... this is a discrete and confidential personal arrangement, nothing to do with the office.'

'We are really disappointed with you, we know the funds came from an account in Middle East, and I am sure it will be proved that the relevant account belongs to House of Al-Zor.' Terry stopped for few moments; 'we can move on if you just admit the position.'

Chris is shocked; not only they knew of his account but also the amount and the sources of funds. He is quiet, he realised that there was very little he could do but to admit it. He played his last card, 'you know Terry that I worked very hard on this project, you yourself praised my work in the email you sent me, and it was copied to Sir Henry as well.'

'Sorry Chris, I did not know at that time what was behind your work. Chuck and Peter noticed the change in your attitude a while ago, you have been arguing to bring the price down, and I felt the same in the closing meeting, but I thought that was your eagerness to close the deal!' Terry's face was serious.

'The deal was well argued and in the benefit of Green Park International, you know the banks were not going to finance their gold project.'

'Look Chris, this meeting is going to be very long if we reincarnate every single detail of the negotiation..., I think you know very well you have broken the fiduciary client trust.'

'I am sorry you feel this way. I have not broken any trust, if Hashim wants to reward me for a successful deal, it is up to him...' then suddenly realising that he had almost admitted the money came from Hashim, 'I mean if he rewards me something, I will declare it to the firm and client. In fact, I will pay it to the firm if you like.'

Anwar realised that Chris had no legs to stand on. 'Chris the game is up, let's move on.'

'I am really disappointed Chris, I still do not believe it but now...I have to find the ways to protect the firm and myself.' Terry's face turned dark. Chris knew if they had so many details, he will not be able to do much. 'Okay, so what do you propose?'

'Do you realise that there could be an enquiry under Money Laundering Act ... and apart from FCA, all kinds of organisations are involved.' Chris is quiet, he needed time to think.

'Chris you have jeopardised the relationship with a very important client. They have been paying huge fees, and owe us quite a large chunk. There is a serious risk of FCA investigation...even Serious Fraud Office could be involved. We need to act quickly.'

'I need time to think.' Chris gave up.

'There is no time.' Terry said in a cold voice. 'I and Sir Henry have come up with this plan...'

'So Sir Henry knows about it?' Chris asked.

'Chris you do not realise the implications, the whole firm could be in serious troubles... we all had to control ourselves when we learnt about it yesterday. Look this is the plan... you return the money to the sender of it in the same bank accounts where it came from which I believe is related to House of Al-Zor... your bank will see the money coming in and out in a space of short time, maybe they will not disclose it to the regulatory authority under Proceeds of Crime Act.' Terry takes a sip of water from the glass in front of him. 'Once the money is gone, you close that account… and yes… absolutely, no word about it, not even to your family!'

While Chris thinking what he had heard, Terry looks at Anwar.
'I have got your resignation letter ready and I can get your P45 and Exit Form as soon as you have signed it.' Anwar takes out a letter from a folder in front of him, and gives it to Chris.
'I hope you realise the position, it is important that we act fast and clean up the mess before it goes out of control… you know what I mean!' Terry's sad face said it all.

They continued to discuss the matter in detail for another hour. Chris left the office with a very sad face. Anwar closed the recording of the meeting in his machine.

A little later in his office, Chris could not concentrate. He tried to tidy up his desk, reply a few emails but his mind was not working. He was still in a state of shock. Then he made up his mind. He told his secretary that he was going to get some files and will be back shortly.

As soon as he arrived home, he rang Hashim. Meina was in her office, he felt better alone. It took a while before he managed to get hold of Hashim. He explained briefly to him what had happened. Hashim was sympathetic. 'What can I do to help you?' Hashim asked him gently.
'Please give me the bank details so that I can transfer the money back to you, I have to trust you to keep the money for me for a while.'
'No problem, if you come to my country I can buy you a bar of gold which you can keep at home, without any account, or in a safe deposit box.'
'At present, I have to sort out this thing so there is no problem at my office, Green Park International and your own position.'

'I understand it completely.' Hashim knew that if this thing was blown, his own stake in Green Park International would come to scrutiny.

'I will be in London in a week or so, perhaps we can meet and discuss the position.'

'Sure, I will keep you updated...obviously, this is absolutely confidential.' Chris pleaded.

'Don't worry Chris, for us this amount is not material at all. I will not even discuss it in our company. It is you who needs to deal with utmost care.'

'I will…I must go.'

'Bye Chris.' Hashim did not show any sign of worries.

'Bye Hashim… and thank you.' Chris pressed the button on his mobile.

Immediately Chris rang his bank and spoke to his account manager. It was Jacques on the other line. He did not know him because most of the time, he dealt with the bank online. Chris explained to him that he needed to transfer the money back urgently to the same bank account where it came from. Jacques was friendly and advised him to do it online. Chris explained to him that a friend of his had given funds to him to buy some property, but the friend needed the funds back urgently for his business cashflow. He also wanted to close this account for personal reasons. Jacques did not buy his explanation but after a few moments, he decided that he will do it. 'We pride ourselves in our clients' service.' Jacques said proudly to Chris. Within a short time, he carried out the transactions and sent him a text message which Chris confirmed immediately. Shortly afterward, Chris retuned to the office.

Next day, there was a meeting in the office of Sir Henry Sheldon at Henry Sheldon LLP. It was the exit interview of Chris Sneale. Sir Henry Sheldon was sitting in his chair behind the desk. The office was in line with the senior partner of a sizeable practice. There were paintings on the wall, mahogany bookcase, antique style large solid wood desk with leather in the middle, a captain's wooden chair with the matching leather.

Chris had signed his resignation letter the day before; he had also gone through the exit procedure: returned the mobile, company credit card, firm's laptop and other items.

Sir Henry looked at Chris who looked like he had not slept the night before. He really felt sorry for this young man who had a bright future ahead of him in the firm. 'Terry and I are really sorry to see you go.' Sir Henry did not show any anger. 'You could have brought this practice down; Chris, the firm's goodwill and very survival are threatened!'
'I really am sorry Sir Henry; I never had any intention to do that. I really hope this unfortunate episode will be forgotten soon.' Chris sounded genuinely apologetic.
'Chris has already returned the money to Al-Zor and closed the relevant account.' Terry said.
'Let's hope that the bank does not disclose it to the regulators.' Sir Henry paused. 'Why did you do it Chris; aren't we paying you enough?'
Chris is quiet; he did not really know what to say. 'No Sir, it is just one of those things, I worked very hard on this project for the benefit of the firm, and did not think that a reward from Hashim will be construed as an immoral payment.'
'Surely, as a lawyer, knowing all the laws and especially our position as guardian of client's trust…. Well let me not get into that detail, I hope you do not consider that the reward was justified.' Sir Henry was disappointed with his reply, and showed his disapproval with his facial expressions.
'No Sir, I really am sorry… as I said, I got carried away, and my judgement got blurred.' Chris admitted his mistake.
'I and Anwar have gone through the procedure with Chris, handover has been smooth. Peter and Chin have taken over between them all the assignments Chris was involved.' Terry did not want the meeting to go too long.
'Chris you had a great future in our firm and you were doing well, Terry always praised you.' Sir Henry softened up.
'I will do my best to protect the name of Henry Sheldon LLP… I have been a loyal employee.'

'Good, if anyone contacts you, of course, you would let us know prior to admitting any wrong doing.' Terry had already asked this before but warned to ensure that he repeats his promise again in front of Sir Henry. 'Of course, I will inform the firm straight away. Since adequate measures have been taken, I do not think we are going to hear anything in this connection in future.'

'Let's hope that is what happens.' Sir Henry looked at Terry who understood that he wanted to have a few words alone with Chris.

Terry got up 'Excuse me Sir; I will be in my office, if you need me.'

'Thanks Terry, I will see you later.' Sir Henry and Terry understood well each other.

'Please pass by my office before leaving the office.' Terry looked at Chris.

'Sure.' Chris was brief.

When Terry had gone, Sir Henry looked at Chris sympathetically, 'what are you going to do now?'

'I am not sure, guess look for another job… I discussed yesterday with Terry and Anwar about the reference.'

'I understand… perhaps, I can speak to them. I do not think we will give any reference for a month or so until the immediate threat has gone, after that, we will see what can be done. Why don't you take a holiday for a few weeks before looking for another job?'

'I can assure you Sir, this matter ends here, no one will ever mention it, and in my opinion, there is no threat whatsoever, the bank account has been closed, the funds back to the originator exactly in the same account where they came from.'

'Fine, that's good…let's hope it stays that way.' Sir Henry got up from his chair and came round close to Chris who also got up from his chair, Sir Henry hugged him. Then in a low voice, he whispered, 'Couldn't you be a little discrete; maybe next year, it would have been you instead of Lenny!'

Chris was startled; he could not believe what he had heard. His mind worked fast and the Christmas party came as a flash in his mind, but he could only say. 'Sir, I don't understand.'

'You do! You are almost the age of my son. In life, one needs to be discrete about the matters which can ruin other peoples' lives.'

Chris stayed quiet while trying to digest what he had heard.
'But let me not keep you, we all make mistakes sometimes in our lives, you are a young man, with a little bit more care and control, you could still make a success of your career.'
'Thank you Sir; most grateful for your understanding.' Chris was glad that the meeting was over.
'Goodbye.' Sir Henry extended his hand. Chris shook his hand with both of his hands. 'Thank you Sir and goodbye,' he was not sure what he felt: relief or disappointment, as he left the office.

In the evening, Chris was back at home early, Meina had not yet come back from work. He had not told her what has been happening in the last two days. She noticed yesterday that he looked very pale and worried. He had told her that he was not feeling very well and that he was rather stressed. Meina knew that in professional life, the stress was a normal occurrence, and a good wife needed to understand it. She did not insist. He remained quiet, lost in thoughts the whole evening. Most of the time, he was on his laptop. Last night, he had pretended to that he fell asleep while his mind was full of worries: what was he going to do? how he was going to break the news to Meina?, humiliation in front of her family. His own father lived in Bristol with a female partner. His mother had remarried after the divorce and lived in Geneva. He was the only child.

He rang his dad and explained to him that he had lost his job. He could not tell him the real reason for the loss of his job. His father who had gone through more serious incidents in his life tried to encourage him, 'at your age Chris, you can find another job easily. You are a smart person, well-educated and a bright lawyer; don't let this setback hold you.'
'Yes dad, I will get over it,' he promised.

'Why don't you and Meina come to Bristol and spend some time with us,' his dad asked him.

'Sure, I would love to; let me speak to Meina, she is not back yet.'

'Good, give my love to her.'

'Will do, thanks dad.' Chris was pleased he spoke to his dad.

He went to Kitchen and poured a glass from the white wine bottle which was normally kept there. He took a big sip while walking to the lounge. His mind felt a little better. Could white wine in cold evening, on stressed mind worked well, he wondered. He started to regain his confidence.

It wasn't long before Meina arrived. She did not notice that he was sitting in the lounge; she went to her bedroom and changed; then she noticed that Chris was back and she went to the lounge. Chris got up when he saw her. He kissed her, 'would you like some white wine?' Chris asked.

'No thanks...you are early?'

'Yeah, I left the office early today.'

'Tell me what's going on? You still look very pale,' she could not wait to find out.

'Oh, nothing...sit down please. Let me tell you.'

Meina sat down, 'okay, shoot.'

'I just lost the job.' Chris voice was lacking any emotion.

'What!! I don't believe it, look Chris I don't like this kind of joke!'

'No darling, I have really lost my job.' Chris' face now showed the sadness which she had seen yesterday as well.

'Please Chris… no, you can't be serious!'

'Look you don't need to repeat McEnroe's dialogue to dramatize…I am serious.'

Meina was in shock now. 'What happened?'

'Well …' Chris collected his thoughts; 'you know this project I have been working for the last few weeks, they did not like my work, there was disagreement which turned sour, and the only option at the end of the day was to resign.' Chris had already planned how he was going to break the news to Meina.

Meina's face changed, finally the news sank in. She is quiet for a few moments, 'when do you leave the company?'

'I already have left, today was my last day. They did not want me to mess around and I did not wish to waste my time.'

'But…' Meina could not speak, 'how is it possible! In twelve hours, you resigned and left the office for good, when did you handover? What about all the cases you have been working on?'

'Look, don't worry… everything is sorted out, I am going to look for another job.' Chris did not want to explain his humiliation at the office.

'How can everything be sorted out… wait a minute you knew it for some time? But it can't be…we only went to look for the property last week. You keep on dropping bombshells!'

'Meina, cool down. I had problems in the office relating to work in Green Park International, and they asked me to leave.' Chris could not keep the suspense any more.

'How can they ask you to leave just like that, I am an HR officer, I know the law, you can sue them for wrongful dismissal; can't you?'

'No I can't…' Chris takes a sigh. 'You remember the money I got from Hashim that is strictly not kosher.'

'I see, so they are accusing you of bribes….God, I don't know what to say.' She put her hands on her head with almost tears in her eyes.

'I did not take any fucking bribe. I did some work for Hashim for which he paid me. In hindsight, that is a conflict of interest, and I should not have done it.' Chris shouted and tried to justify his action.

'So what happens to the money?'

'I had to return it to Hashim; I will claim it back when the time is right.'

'So no job, no money, no Spanish house… God what a change within twenty four hours!!' Meina was in despair.

'Don't worry darling, I will get another job, the money is safe with Hashim; everything is going to be okay.' Chris was not sure himself but he tried to calm his wife.

Meina was not satisfied with the reply and started crying. Chris himself was worried, could not see her cry, he got up from his chair and hugged her an kissed her affectionately on her cheeks, 'it is not so serious Meina, you will see everything will be alright in a few days... let's go out for a meal somewhere.'

'No, I really don't feel like going out; besides, I had defrozen some fish this morning, it will go bad.'

Before Chris could say anything she went into the kitchen. Chris went to the desk in the lounge which he used to use for work. He took out a visitor cards book and started looking at the cards to see if he could use any of his contacts. He took his laptop and started looking at some of the jobsites specialising in legal recruitment. Then he realised his CV was not up-to-date, he needed to revise it. He took out his old CV from a file in the drawer and started updating his CV.

Chapter 10

Days passed, Chris could not find a suitable job. His earlier confidence
that he will find a reasonable job quickly was gone. Gradually, he became
quite frustrated with his unsuccessful search. He also remembered often
what Sir Henry had said about being discrete in life, he definitely knew
about Sharon and Lenny; he also knew that it was he who was in the
filing room watching that bloody episode. It was because of him poor
Lenny tried to delete the footage from the CCTV. He felt guilty; he felt
he was almost responsible for Lenny's career being ruined. Was it God's
justice that he himself was in such deep shit? He wished he wouldn't
have been there. He also remembered Sir Henry's advice to take some
time off. He understood well that they wanted to see if there was any
sign of any malpractice or hint of investigation from the client, FCA or
any other regulatory bodies. If they did, his fate would probably be
sealed. Otherwise, the matter will die down. Maybe Henry Sheldon
would realise that he increased their billing substantially; maybe they will
ask him to come back.

Finally, Chris decided to visit Bristol to spend the weekend with his
father. Meina also wanted to go but she decided that Chris would relax
better alone with his dad, local pubs, football and squash. She could
spend some more time with her mum. She also felt that his step mother-
in-law did not really like her. But the main reason was her mother's
temple visit for her father's death anniversary, when all the family went
into special service in the big temple in Willesden. She always found her

mother's devotion for her father quite remarkable. Her father, even after death, played a big part in her mother's life.

Weekend came, Chris went to Bristol to spend it with his dad and step mother while Meina went to her mother's home. The very evening Terry, Sharon and Anwar and his wife Shabnam were invited for dinner at Sir Henry's home in Greenwich. Simon Randall and his wife could not make it; they were visiting their daughter in New Zealand.

Sir Henry's house was a piece of antiques in itself. It was an old Victorian house, with a good architecture and special features. It was decorated in old English style. Good quality Mahogany and red wood furniture, Iranian carpets, old paintings, some of them from old masters, crystal chandeliers, large hard wood bookshelves.

At the table were Sir Henry and his guests. Sharon did not really like these formal dinners with comparatively old people but she knew that for her husband's career, it was necessary. The food and the wine were of the highest quality. It seemed that all the ingredients came from Piccadilly's exclusive food shop, Fortnum & Mason which was known to be the best in London. They were in the middle of their main course. There was also Amara, who came to help in the house cleaning and other work on a daily basis for couple of hours, and also helped in cooking and serving when they had guests around. She also brought her sister when there was a big party. She stayed in the kitchen and came from time to time to assist.

Terry had a piece of meat cooked in African sauces. 'It is delicious, what is it?'
'It is lamb cooked in African way, today Amara prepared it; she said that their food had a lot of French influence.' Pamela replied.
'Oh yes, it seems to be a good mixture of Indian and French cooking.' Shabnam added.

Shabnam was a middle aged wife of Anwar; they had been in the UK for long time and were adapted to English culture, even though, she mostly dressed in Indian clothes. She was wearing a Sari.

'How do you like it, Sharon?' Sir Henry looked at Sharon.

'Oh, me… I love trying all kinds of new dishes, it is my sense of adventure but I must say it is really nice.' Sharon put up her seducing smile.

Sir Henry also smiled, 'good'.

Soon they were having sweet which everyone seemed to like as well. Then they all moved to the lounge where Amara served them coffee and cognac. Shabnam declined cognac. 'You would love it Shabnam, special from Harrods; we bought it at Christmas.' Sir Henry looked at Shabnam.

'No Henry, I had some wine that was enough alcohol for one day… I don't really drink.'

After a few minutes, Sir Henry asked Terry. 'Terry, did you hear anything from Chris?'

'No, I guess he is trying to find a new job. It is not easy to find the right job quickly these days.' Terry took a sip of cognac.

'I did not have anyone ask for his reference, it is rather strange. Many times, agencies ring and try to find about a person discretely.' Anwar said.

'We have to be careful for a little while more. I have not heard so far from any regulatory bodies.'

'Of course, these days, a number of companies just confirm employment dates and do not express any opinion.' Anwar explained.

'Yes, I think the trend is from States where there have been a number of lawsuits.' Terry remarked.

There was a silence for a few moments, 'Any news from Lenny?' Sir Henry looked at Terry. Sharon's face slightly changed when she heard it but no one noticed. 'No, I believe he is in Melbourne, I recently met Raymond Baxter who seemed to think that he was doing okay.' Terry looked at Anwar with an enquiring face.

'No, I have not heard from him or about him for that matter.' Anwar added.

'I think we lost two good people one after another, as Oscar Wilde will put it, 'to lose one is bad but losing two is negligence.' Sir Henry lightened up the conversation. While they were laughing, he said, 'let's hope this trend will not continue, it is time to find a few good solicitors like Lenny and Chris.'

'I am on lookout; I met a few people in the recent seminar and dropped a hint to one solicitor who is with one of the top five firms.' Terry pointed out.

'I have been speaking to some headhunters. They are going to send me the names of two but they are well settled in the jobs but with right sort of package, can be moved.' Anwar updated them.

'Good, we need the firm to grow.'

In the meantime, Amara came into the lounge. 'Would anyone like some more cognac?' She picked up the bottle.

'Just a drop for me,' said Sir Henry.

'Yes please.' Terry said. 'You are driving right?' He looked at Sharon.

'Yeah, sure as usual!' Sharon smiled.

'Not for me. Thanks.' Anwar said.

Sir Henry looked at the women who were largely ignored since last half an hour or so. They formed their own small group and were talking about the latest fashion, films and children, while their husbands brought their office to home.

The same evening, a few miles away, Meina was in the temple with Leena and her brother, Balak. The temple is situated in Willesden. It is made of stones, the architecture is that found in old traditional temples in India. The building is the most famous Indian temple in the UK. Balak has been carrying a large basket of Indian sweets, and Meina had been carrying a basket of fruits, coconuts and others, also some rice. Leena had a small basket of flowers. The priest received them with greetings. He knew the family as the frequent visitor to the temple, and also yearly special puja for Meina's late father. Balak was wearing an Indian white trouser and a white kurta while the women were in simple sarees.

The ceremony took place, the fruits were placed at the feet of devtas and some sweets from the basket were placed near the Devtas' feet. After about an hour of puja and rituals, Leena offered the pundit an envelope containing cash for his services. He took it and blessed them, and put the tilak on their foreheads. The happy and spiritually charged family returned home knowing that they had done the right thing for Leena's late husband and the father of her children.

Irena joined them at home for the dinner. She could not join them for the puja. Balak served the drinks, sweet white wine as aperitif. The meal was going to be a mix of Indian curry, kebabs and Indian version of spaghetti (pasta cooked with masala sauce, a favourite of Balak).

Irena was a young woman who looked after her body. She was not very pretty but very attractive due to her shapely body, and she looked good in most of the clothes. She also knew how to do a fine make up, She had a nice smile with dimple; Balak loved those dimples. While at dinner, Irena noticed that Balak was still in the white kurta and trousers. 'Are you going to stay in your pyjamas?' She teased him.
'Well, it means I don't have to change when we go to bed!' he smiled.
'This curry and this Indian spaghetti will definitely keep you awake, God, it is hot!'
'You see the Indians are all hot people, everything about us is hot! You can touch me if you like.' Balak was in a playful mood.
'Children, wait till you are alone!' Leena told them.
'Oh Mumiji, let them talk like that, it is nice; Chris has been such a bore recently.' Meina was happy to have a change of scenery.
'I have not seen Chris for a while, where is he?' Irena asked.
'He is in Bristol visiting his dad and step-mum, normally, he would have been here.' Meina explained.
'I see.'

'Chris lost his job recently, and at present, looking for another one, Meina spent a long time in temple, praying for his job.' Balak grinned.
'Don't be silly, I was praying for dad... You should be helping your brother-in-law instead of making fun of him.' Meina defended her husband.
'Stop it.' Leena ordered Balak.
'I was only lightening up the conversation; of course, I want to help Chris. I already spoke to my solicitor, their firm is rather small but he is going to let me know. In fact, he heard of Chris in the newspaper, a while ago.'
'Good.' Leena was happy.
'I can speak to my boss, can he speak Italian? They have a lot of contacts in Italy; I think an Italian speaking lawyer will be very handy.' Irena offered her contribution to the family.

Not far from Wimbledon Championship court, a British Indian family with cosmopolitan ingredients, continued to enjoy cosmopolitan food.

Just over a hundred miles away, the same evening Chris was playing squash with Dennis, in the local leisure centre. It was a nice centre with swimming pool, sauna, gym and indoor tennis courts. Denis was a fitness fanatic and was in good shape. He was finance manager in Bristol University. For his late fifties, he played squash well.
'Are you going to let me beat you, come on man!' shouted Dennis.
'God, I am trying! Have you been practising all the time?' Chris asked.
'No, I have not been.' Dennis hit the ball harder, the ball died at the corner. Chris ran but the ball was too low and he hit the wall with his racket.
'Seven: four.' Dennis said with a smile as he served the ball. Soon the score was eleven: four, and the game over.
'Would you like another game, son?' Dennis asked.
'Not today, I think I had enough, I need to get fit again.' Chris looked tired.

A few minutes later, they were sitting in the small café which served healthy drinks, teas coffees and light snacks.

'Chris you are looking very tired… what's the matter?'

'I don't know, I guess I am a little depressed, I am trying my best to get another job but it does not seem to work.'

Dennis took a big sip of the orange juice, 'tell me one thing, how did your firm know about your arrangements with this Arab guy anyway?'

'That is also mystery, I keep analysing it in my mind every day but it does not make any sense.'

'Did anyone in the firm know about your arrangements?' Dennis enquired.

'Absolutely not, I have been extremely careful … even Meina did not know about it until the day before.' Chris showed his desperation. 'No one in the office knew. Meina did not know… Hashim could not possibly do it… bank maybe, but if they did it, would normally come through some regulatory body FCA, Fraud Squad…?'

Dennis looked around to ensure no one was interested in their conversation, 'but son, the office have to know from somewhere!?'

'Yes dad, I can't really ask anyone, the less you talk about it, better it is.' Chris said it in a low voice.

'May be the bank… but you closed the account, they probably would not take any further action especially the funds went back to the sender?'

'It really does not matter, does it?'

'I suppose not… did you have a fight in the office?'

'No dad, let's forget it, the guy I did not get along well, left a long time ago. In fact, I understand, he went to Australia.'

'Maybe he came back to London or on a visit here!'

'Not likely, I would have learnt if he was around.'

'Okay, don't worry too much, you need to get fit again, put your mind into something else. I wouldn't mind being a grandad!' Dennis' face showed his fatherly affection for his only son, in fact, the only child.

'Meina's family is also hinting it … how can I start a family in the current circumstances!'

'I know you will get a job soon, you should take the whole thing out of your system, drain it out. I am going to speak to one of the professors; his son is a solicitor with one of the top firms.'

'No dad; let me continue my own search, it is not going to work, at my level, this will lower my image.'

'Alright, let's finish the drink, we need to get back. Yvonne will be waiting for us; she has booked the table at the restaurant.'

A few minutes later, a fit father and his not so fit son left the leisure centre.

Time was passing, days to weeks; Chris could not find a suitable job. He was getting very frustrated. All his contacts could not do anything. His father's contact did show some interest and discussed the possibility of him joining the Bristol office of a large practice, but the level was too junior; besides, Meina's job in London, it did not seem right. He continued with his efforts but did not get anywhere. As a result of his frustrations, his temper became erratic and he started having rows at home with Meina. He also stopped meeting his friends, some of them worked in Henry Sheldon LLP who also avoided him. Hashim had been to London for two days but did not find time to meet him. Chris was so disappointed. He started having second thoughts about Hashim and the funds entrusted to him. He did not want the funds in his own name yet, just in case, the saga came back. He wanted to make sure he got a proper job.

Meina tried her best to live with Chris' frustrations. She used her contacts to get him a job but no success. She also felt that she was becoming the victim of his frustrations. Chris was becoming moody day by day. One evening, when she returned from the office, she found Chris drinking heavily.

'Chris what are you doing? You are going to damage your health,' she warned him.

'I feel sorry for myself. It is waste of my time trying to get the job... I am so bored.' Chris replied.

'I spoke to Balak; he was saying that perhaps you can join him. He said that he can start another pharmacy with more cosmetics and general stuff, a bit like Boots really.'

'You know I am a lawyer and not a pharmacist, what are you talking about?' Chris was slightly annoyed.

'I mean not a pharmacy, more like a shop where they sell men and women's make up, perfume and other cosmetics. It is a business. Balak thinks that there is a scope to make a small chain of shops.' Meina explained patiently.

'No Meina, I need to stay in my own profession; I don't know what's the matter, but they seemed to have blacklisted me!'

Meina comes close to him and kisses him. 'Don't worry darling, things will get better. Maybe we should go to the USA, I can ask for a transfer in my firm and I am sure you can get a job easily there. Apparently, there is a strong demand for the lawyers over there, particularly those, with commercial exposure like yours.'

'In the US, the laws are different but similar to a certain degree... but why suddenly USA?'

'Oh I met Chuck the other day in the City. He mentioned that there were a lot of opportunities in the USA at the moment.'

'You met Chuck, how come you never told me before!?'

'I was having lunch with an office friend in a restaurant, he happened to pass by and we talked a few minutes.'

'You should keep away from all the people from Henry Sheldon, they are no longer my friends, the way they treated me!' Chris' face showed sign of unpleasantness.

'Sorry darling, I could not avoid him, he came to our table and talked a few minutes, Rolanda thought he was really interesting.'

'You shouldn't beg jobs for me; I will deal with it myself. Maybe instead of buying a property in Spain, I will form an offshore company and invest funds in London and start a property company.' Chris voice was cold.

Meina did not wish to continue this conversation so she changed the topic. 'Let's go out for a meal.'

A few minutes later they left the flat.

Another week passed, Chris became more and more frustrated for lack of his success. He did attend one interview but was disheartened when the agency did not take it further. He suspected that Henry Sheldon LLP was not giving him a good reference. So his chances of getting a job looked slim day by day. Chris and Meina started arguing about small things. Meina tried her best to be as understanding wife as she could but she was working and had her own pressure of work, and on occasions, frustrations. Chris did not want to meet anyone. He was sure that the immediate choice was to start his own practice or get into properties. He decided that he wanted to get his money from Hashim, so he rang him. Chris decided to spend the weekend with his mum and on Monday, he will meet Hashim and open a bank account over there. Chris discussed with Meina and they decided that they needed to be careful with money now, so he went alone.

Saturday morning, Chris left for Geneva, Meina was planning to visit her mum in the evening, when in the afternoon, she received a call. It was from Sharon Hamilton. 'Hi Meina, this is Sharon.' Meina heard the cheerful voice of Sharon.
'Nice to hear from you.' Meina also sounded friendly.
'Listen, one of our friends cannot join us for dinner, so I thought of you, I hope you do not mind such a short notice, I apologise!'
'That's okay, Sharon, we do the same sometimes. We know each other, there is no formality but Chris has gone to Geneva to meet his mum.'
'Oh, I see… Meina, why don't you come?' Sharon asked in a friendly way.
'I… I was thinking to go to my mum; besides, it will look odd without Chris.'
'Don't be silly, what is odd about it? Chris is having a good time with his family, you could do the same!'
'I don't know…you know since Chris left Henry Sheldon…..'

Sharon interrupted, 'look we are still friends. Terry always liked Chris, he always praised his work!'
Meina was quiet for a moment. She was thinking it could not harm, besides, Terry probably could help Chris in the job or for the reference, 'alright, what time?'
'Say, about seven?'
'Fine, I will see you, thanks Sharon.' Meina tried to sound more friendly than they really were.
'Bye, see you.' Sharon disconnected.

Meina was thinking, how come suddenly Sharon rang! Was it a coincidence that Chris was not there, should she ring Chris, and tell him about it? Anyway, her meeting with Hamiltons will clear the air and perhaps help Chris in his job search. She decided that her decision was right; there was no need to bother Chris.

In the evening, Meina was at Hamilton's house in Mill Hill. It was a low key affair. There were two couples, Peter Cooper and his wife Brenda Cooper, Linda Hammond and her husband Neil. The food was good and it was a seated dinner. Rebecca was not there; she had helped Sharon in preparation of food, but had left before the guests arrived. Sharon received Meina as though, they were close friends. Meina was happy to receive such a warm welcome. She was also hoping to see Chuck, but Sharon explained that he was invited by one of his friends at the US Embassy dinner. Surprisingly, during the course of dinner, they did not talk about the office; no one mentioned Chris either.

It was nice evening and Meina was relaxed. Short time after dinner, Peter and Brenda left; Linda and Neil were still there. Meina also wanted to leave but Sharon insisted for another coffee.
'So your husband is enjoying Geneva?' said Linda.
'I am not sure, I don't think he likes very much his stepfather,' replied Meina.

'You guys are catching bankers in the bonus league!' remarked Neil.
'Not, really, I am an HR person, 25% is about the maximum as opposed
to 200% of the bankers; most of the years, for me it is 15%.' Meina
explained.
Terry looked at Meina, 'we are not gamblers, these people gamble with
other people's money and get rewarded.'
'Neil nodded, 'I agree.'

They continued to talk and after a while, Linda and Neil also left. Meina
looked at her watch. She did not really have to do anything at home. She
was enjoying the cosy atmosphere: the good food, excellent wine and
smiling faces with some good humour; it made her relaxed. After a short
while, when she looked at her watch again, 'Oh… why don't you stay
overnight, we got plenty of room; Max is at the boarding school.' Sharon
offered.
'That's very kind of you, no; it wouldn't take me very long to get back,
not much traffic at this time of night.'
'What's the position with Chris, is he alright?' asked Terry.
'He is a bit depressed that is why he is gone to his mum in Geneva. On
the job front, no luck so far!' Meina was pleased that he asked about
Chris. In the meantime, telephone rang and Sharon left to answer the
phone in the hall. Now Terry and Meina were alone.

'You know Meina why Chris left the job?' Terry did not want to say that
he was fired. Meina felt a little embarrassed before she could reply, Terry
came closer and touched her shoulder. 'Sorry my dear, I did not wish to
embarrass you!' Meina enjoyed the touch. Suddenly, she realised that that
they were alone in the room. With a handsome man in a room, after
plenty of good food and wine, the mind drifts and the physical desire
takes over. She looked into Terry's eyes and said innocently. 'I know the
reason but perhaps you could help him.'

Terry could not read her eyes; he thought it is always difficult to read the
signals from the eyes of Asian women. He took his hand away from her
shoulder and said, 'of course, I would like to help him, I always thought

very highly of him. Sometimes, an error of judgement can cause a lot of problems and headaches.'
Meina looked at him again into his eyes and brought her hand forward and put on Terry's hand, 'I am sure you want to help me. I will be ever so grateful!' Meina put a little emphasis on 'me'.

Terry felt the heat of her hand; she is really hot, he thought. This brown woman in silky dress, he felt like taking her to the bedroom, and discover her interiors. He wondered what it would be like to have a threesome, God that will be so great! White chocolate and golden brown chocolate; I bet I can make both of them happy. Meina also suddenly felt the heat of his hand. Terry was about ten years older than Chris but his hands were as warm if not warmer. Thinking that Sharon could come back any time, she took her hand away gently. 'I will see what I can do,' Terry said, wondering why he never paid much attention to her in the previous meetings.

In the meantime, Sharon came back to the lounge. She intentionally went to the toilet after finishing the telephone to give them more time to be alone. She noticed that Terry was sitting close to the sofa towards Meina's side. She felt her plan was working!

After about half an hour, Meina left Hamiltons' house happy with the knowledge that she had rediscovered true friends in Hamiltons. That night when Meina was in bed she was not sure if she was thinking of Terry or Chris?

The weekend passed, Chris came back on Tuesday instead of Monday evening, as was planned. He had started forming an offshore company in which the shareholder and the director will be nominees and not him; even though, he will beneficially own the company. He will also act as an agent of that company in the UK. In spite of Swiss efficiency, he could not get it done in one day. Hashim had promised to transfer the funds to the new company's bank account so that it could not be related to Chris.

Chris remained busy the whole week trying to find a job and his new company being set up in Switzerland. He began to feel the financial pressure. One modest salary of Meina was coming in, expenses were more or less same as before and it made a big dent in his savings; now the additional expenses of travelling and setting up company in Switzerland. Meina found that he was always on the telephone or on his lap top, and he hardly spoke to her. In the evenings, often he will go to play squash with some of his friends or socialise with some business contacts in the hope of finding a job. She felt quite unhappy with the situation and being neglected.

One lunch time, Meina received a call from Sharon asking her to meet for lunch. She said that she was in the City; Terry went to a meeting with a client. Meina gladly accepted enjoying attention of a beautiful and influential woman. They met in a small restaurant in the City. While they were having their lunch they continued to talk. 'It is nice atmosphere seeing all these City's people in their business suits!' Sharon remarked. 'Yeah, it is but one hour is really not enough for lunch, I tend to have many times sandwiches in the office.'
'How the accounting world is doing?' Sharon asked her.
'Good, our firm is really growing. I am very busy visiting universities, interesting young graduates, sometimes, I interview newly qualified as well.'
When the lunch was nearly over, Sharon asked, 'how is Chris, any luck with the job?'
'No, he is going to Switzerland again tomorrow, would be away for couple of nights.'
'I think he is looking for comfort in his mum's arms.' Sharon laughed.
Meina did not want to explain to her that he was setting up a company. 'I suppose when in stress, it is the family you rely on.'

'Of course.... I was just joking... listen Meina, why don't you come to our place tomorrow, it would be really nice. I feel quite lonely sometimes, Max is in the boarding school and my parents live in Brighton. They do not visit enough; my sister with her husband is in Montreal, I think they are going to settle down there.'

'I have just been to your home a few days ago.., I visit my brother and mum when Chris is not around.'

'I am sure you can see them at the weekend, please do come, it would be nice, otherwise Terry will probably work and I will watch TV.

Meina thought for a moment. She had not told Chris that she was with Sharon at the weekend when he was away. 'Can I call you tomorrow morning?'

'That's fine; actually I also wanted to show you a painting by a famous Indian artist. I brought it at home; we got couple for sale in our gallery.'

'I do not know much about paintings, 'Mona Lisa' and 'Nightwatch' probably, no more!'

'You do not need to know about paintings to really appreciate them. For most people, a painting is good if it looks nice to them and pleasant to their eyes.... Besides, this painting has got certain Indian words; maybe you can explain it to me.'

Meina is quiet 'Okay if you insist, I can come; are you sure Terry wouldn't mind?'

'Not at all, on the contrary, he would like it. He was quite impressed last time... he was really good in!!!! You know...you must have influenced him in the right place!!'

'I see now the real reason! My magic spell makes you happy in bed!!'
Meina laughed.
Sharon smiled.

After a short while, two 'good friends' left the restaurant happy liking each other.

Next evening, Meina arrived at Sharon's home. She noticed that Terry was not there. Sharon was in good mood and wearing a light midi dress 'You look beautiful!' remarked Meina, 'where is Terry?'

'Oh he is a little late. He should be back in a few minutes.' Sharon replied. 'Hang on, you said, I am looking beautiful! Let's both go in front of the mirror…you look so sexy!!'

Meina smiled. She had put a light material trouser with a tight silk shirt, showing all her shapely body; she had also put on some make up. She could be anywhere from Mediterranean. 'I am your mirror; you can see yourself in me.' Meina showed her sense of humour.

'Alright, let's say we both look beautiful, Terry will have a difficult time choosing between us!!' Sharon showed her broad mindedness.

'I am sure he is going to choose his wife, men always do!' Meina laughed.

Sharon opened a bottle of Champagne which was in an ice bucket in the lounge.

'What is the occasion?' Meina asked.

'We do not need an occasion to drink champagne. Besides, I had a really good day at the gallery.' Sharon poured the Champagne in flute glass and gave it to Meina.

'Thanks.' Meina said while Sharon poured one glass for her. 'Cheers' they both said together.

They talked about the weather, the problem in the Middle East for a few minutes. 'Let me show you the painting.' Sharon got up and left the lounge.

Meina looked at the lounge. She thought it was really well decorated but then Sharon was an artistic person, she made things around her as beautiful. Soon Sharon was back with two paintings. 'These both are from a famous Indian painter called Hussain, do you know him?' Sharon showed the paintings to Meina.

'I heard his name, one of Balak's friends once mentioned that these are becoming very popular among the rich Indians in the UK.'

'Yes, they are quite valuable. In fact, there seems to be quite an interest by other British people. Can you read what is written in this painting?' Sharon asked.

'Sorry, I am not sure, it seems like 'Luxmi' and few other letters… these painters have their own language!'

'Their bottom is just like yours, did you model it for him!?' Sharon played with her.

'Let me see the difference.' Meina walked quickly towards Sharon's back, 'no it is very much like yours!' Meina claimed.

Both continued to drink the fine champagne and chat until there was some noise at the entrance. Terry and Chuck entered the house smiling. 'Hi ladies, you look smashing!' Chuck kissed both of them on their cheeks, Terry followed.

'You guys don't look so bad either,' Sharon looked at them seducingly. 'Champagne?' she asked.

'Yes please, never say no to Champagne.' Chuck replied. Sharon served them, and they all raised their glasses 'Cheers.'

They started talking, and in a short while, they were on the dinner table. It was a candle lit dinner for four. The atmosphere was nice; all of them in good mood and the food was also good. Sharon did not ask Rebecca to help; she wanted to keep the evening intimate. They continued to enjoy the dinner. When sorbet was served 'What a splendid sorbet, it is really excellent!' Chuck could not help himself.

'The taste is in the mood, my dear fellow!' Terry said. 'Just like the beauty is in the eyes of the beholder,' they all laughed.

'Sure I am in good mood but then then who will not be, surrounded by such beautiful people!' Chuck looked at Meina and Sharon.

'Flattery will get you everywhere.' Meina replied then she blushed thinking she was too familiar without her husband being there. She decided to keep Chris 'away' for the evening.

'We are looking forward to it.' Terry looked straight into her eyes.

After a few minutes, the dinner was over. They sat on the sofa and continued with some more champagne. Sharon suddenly got up and brought the painting in front of both men, 'you guys are going to be the judges…tell us whose bottom does it look like, Meina's or mine?' Sharon asked Chuck and Terry.

'Well, you girls need to show your bottoms then we can decide.' Terry said; Chuck nodded.

'I thought you had already seen it!' Sharon said, 'but let's show it to you again.' She takes Meina's hand, and they both stand in front of them showing their back. Terry wanted to grab Meina's bottom straight away, with such close proximity and plenty of champagne and a real treat! 'I can't make up my mind.' Chuck looked closely. 'I think let's leave the decision till after the dance.'

Sharon immediately moved towards the CD player, 'What a brilliant idea!' she put slow rhythm music on. She came towards them and took Terry's hand and they both started dancing. Soon Chuck took Meina's hand and they joined the other couple. You look beautiful!' Terry came close to Sharon. She did not reply, just smiled. Chuck was amazed by Meina's sexuality. His blood pressure went higher as soon as he had touched her. 'You dance well.' Meina remarked.

'Not really, I am lost in you; you are such a remarkable lady!'

'Thank you.' Meina said.

After a few minutes, they changed the partners; Terry was now dancing with Meina and Chuck with Sharon. Both couples enjoyed the dance and appreciated the generous beautiful partners. 'I miss you Sharon!' Chuck whispered into Sharon's ears. She did not reply, looked at him and smiled.

Terry could not control himself and his hands moved from Meina's back to her bottom. After a few moments, she teased him 'Are you trying to work out the painting!?'

'Yeah, that was it … I needed to be sure of it before deciding!' Terry this time squeezed her bottom. Meina did not object.

On the next song, Sharon put the light a little dimmer. Both couples continued to dance. They changed once again but were back to Terry with Meina, and Chuck with Sharon. Chuck was careful with Sharon but once he noticed Terry taking liberties with Meina, he decided to have a go as well. Sharon did not object, perhaps both women were in a mood to be generous with their partners.

In the semi darkness, hands moved from the bottom to the front discretely, discovering each other. Each couple was busy with their own partner. When Terry's fingers tried to enter in Meina's trousers, she had to politely stop him. She took his hand and put it on her shoulder which slipped to her breast; she did not want to be too old fashioned so she let it stay there. Terry thought she was one of the sexiest persons he had ever been!! Chuck and Sharon, of course, had discovered each other before, so there was nothing new but rediscovering has its own taste which they both seemed to enjoy.

It was late at night and the time to go. Meina had not had sex with Chris for a while, she was burning inside. Her own frustrations and the drinks, had allowed Terry to take more liberties than she would normally have allowed any other men. Sharon had a great time, apart from enjoying the masculine touch of Chuck and his strong hands; she was pleased that her plan was working!

In a short while, two cars moved from Mill Hill towards Central London. Chuck and Meina were driving their cars. Chuck followed her and they arrived in Kensington; both cars stopped. Meina got out of her car and waited for Chuck near the entrance of her apartment block who parked his car nearby and got out of it. 'What a wonderful evening.' Chuck came close to her.
'Yes, it was, thanks to you and Terry…you did not need to escort me, I would have been okay.'
'No my dear, at this time of night, I could not possibly.' Chuck replied.

Meina was still hot, they looked at each other. 'You will forgive me if I do not ask you in?' Meina controlled her desires, and collected the courage and discipline to say it.

'No Meina… anything you do will not displease me,' he put his hands on her shoulder. They kissed a long passionate kiss; suddenly, Meina took her lips off, 'Sorry Chuck, I got to go.'

'Okay Meina…Thank you for a splendid evening.'

'Good night Chuck.' Meina waved her hand and walked into her apartment block.

'Goodnight.' Chuck said, and waited till she disappeared in the building.

That night, Terry, after so many starters, could not be very hungry for the main course; so after a quick outburst, he fell asleep. Sharon did not mind since she was so happy with her plan's success. Before she could devise her future plan, she also fell asleep. Chuck when arrived at his hotel also fell asleep quickly having had too much of everything: food, drinks, dance and close encounters with two very beautiful ladies. Poor Meina was alone and frustrated in her flat. Both men had ignited her; she wanted Chuck to come up but could not say it. Chris was too far. She could not help thinking about Terry, a serious man but could be like a teenager. If Sharon was not around, he would have made love to her there and then in the lounge. Then it was Chuck, the strong man, not as smooth as Terry but nevertheless, could arouse any woman! She moved from one side to the other but could not sleep. Then she remembered something which always made her sleep. Her fingers moved on her body, the places where Terry and to a lesser degree, Chuck had touched. She kept on thinking about Terry and sometimes Chuck; Chris never appeared in that equation!! It wasn't long before she had a climax, and finally, she also fell asleep.

Chapter 11

A week passed. Chris was back from Switzerland. His company was set up, the funds were transferred in; Hashim was man of his word. He already put a deposit of one of the properties. Since he was not getting any right offers for the jobs, he had decided to concentrate on property. He started spending his time in property search. Occasionally, he will speak to Hashim who was still friendly with him. Chris tried to persuade him to invest some of his money in his property business which he promised to consider. Chuck met Meina at a lunch in the City and left for New York. His work in London was almost complete. In Green Park International, Wolfie fired Alan Davis after learning from his auditors/advisers and one of the directors that they sold out to Hashim Al-Zor rather cheaply. A new CFO was appointed. However, the relationship with Henry Sheldon LLP was not affected.

Meina casually mentioned to Chris that she had been with Sharon over the weekend. Chris was too excited about his new property venture, did not show much interest except saying, 'be careful, that woman is a bitch!' Meina disregarded his caution, as she and Sharon had even come closer.

One day, Sharon was near Marble Arch. There is a famous electronic shop which probably was started by an ex-cop. It has all kinds of modern gadgets: listening devices, microphone in pen, hidden cameras in various shapes, cameras able to take pictures in dark etc. She was in the shop looking at various gadgets. A salesman came to her, 'can I help you madam?'

'I am looking for a hidden camera to take some pictures. You see it is my son's birthday and I wish to make a video without them knowing.' Sharon replied.

'Of course, you want to catch them off guard or maybe going for the TV programme for two hundred fifty quid (reference to a TV programme in which they give two hundred fifty pounds for any clip used in the programme).'

'Yes, something like that.'

'But I am afraid, our cameras and recording devices will cost you a lot more!'

'It's okay; I can use it in my shop afterward, so it will be a business expense.'

The salesman showed her a few cameras and briefly explained its workings. After a short while, Sharon bought one unit and took it home. At home, she tried the camera and its components. It was quite easy to use. She put the hidden camera in the lounge and its component in the bedroom and took some pictures. They seem to work well. A vicious smile came on her face. Now how she was going to get Meina to her place alone? She knew Chris was back. She moved the cameras and the control unit, and hid it in her wardrobe where she knew no one will touch it.

In the evening, Sharon rang Meina. But it was Chris who picked up the phone. 'Hi Sharon.'

'Hello Chris, I thought I was ringing Meina?'

'It is her phone, she is in the bathroom.'

'Alright, I will call her later.' Sharon said.

'What's the hurry, can I speak to you for a minute?' Chris said.

'Of course.'

'I haven't seen you for a long time.'

'I know, why don't you come to our place sometimes with Meina?'

'I will…you see Sharon, I am almost starting a new life…I am in property business now.'

'Good, I knew you had many talents.'

'I wish to buy a few inexpensive paintings for couple of my properties; I am going to rent these out.'

'Sure, you can come to the gallery any time.'

'But I wanted to see you as well; can we go to the lunch after?' Chris tried to sound friendly.

Sharon is quiet for a few seconds. 'Okay you are on!'

'Alright then, I will meet you tomorrow at lunch, say one?'

'That's fine.'

'See you.'

Chris and Sharon were in a bar where they also served light meals. They were drinking red wine and had light pasta dishes.

'I am a new person now, full of confidence; I have already bought two properties and plan to go big soon.'

'I am glad, you do look better.' Sharon tried to please him.

They continued to talk for a while. It was nearly an hour, Sharon looked at her watch.

''Are you in a rush?' Chris asked.

'Not really, but need to get back to the gallery, one of the director's wives wanted to look at some of the paintings.'

Chris took her hand in his, 'Sharon, how much I like you if you knew.'

Sharon smiled. 'Liar, with such a beautiful wife who would want to be with anyone else!'

'She is nice but I really have a crush on you, you know it!' Chris put a little pressure on her hand.

'Why don't you come with Meina at the weekend to our place…I am sure we can all be good friends.' Sharon looked into his eyes meaningfully.

'I would love to… but this weekend Hashim is coming and I have to meet him, he is going to invest in my company.' Chris was surprised with her friendly way; he put his hands on her lap where he could feel the great warmth!

Sharon knew where his hands were but did not move; her mind worked fast. 'Oh that's pity, perhaps another weekend.'

'Sure, would love to.' Chris moved his hand on her lap and felt the sudden heat on his hand. Sharon thought, the guy never learns, still to his old tricks, falling for anything under the skirt. She still did not move. Chris thought that she was getting into the right mood, he had perfect thing to cool that oven; he brought his mouth towards her. She gently put her hand on his mouth, 'it is too early Chris!'

'Okay, perhaps another time.' Chris was still happy.

Sharon did not say anything but smiled. Chris could not read it. Then she looked at her watch again.

Soon Chris paid the bill, and they left the restaurant.

On Friday evening, when Meina got back from the office she found Chris working hard on his laptop. He had been shortlisting the properties and preparing a small business plan to show Hashim the following day. 'Hi.' Meina said in a loud voice.

'I can hear you.' Chris was busy on computer.

'How are you?'

'Okay... busy, need to get ready for tomorrow.'

'What is it tomorrow?'

'I need to meet Hashim in the evening. I am preparing a business plan; I might have a long meeting.'

'But tomorrow we are supposed to go with Balak. He and Irena want to take us out for a meal in a Polish restaurant.'

'Sorry; I am far too busy... perhaps next week.' Chris raised his eyes from his laptop.

'They are going to be disappointed.'

'What is there to be disappointed, the restaurant is not going to go anywhere… basically, there is no special occasion?' Chris went back to looking at his laptop.

'You don't realise, in my family, the relationship matters….my mum is going to be disappointed as well!'

Chris continued to be busy in his work, his mind was lost in figures, he was regretting why he did not ask an accountant to prepare it for him.

'Look… I said to you this deal is very important for me, if Hashim invests the money I will be doing very well!'

'But you can meet him on Sunday?' Meina argued.

Chris looked at her angrily 'Why can't you bloody understand …ring your brother …next week will be fine.'

Meina did not like his angry looks, and left the lounge disappointed. Chris went back to work out why it will take five years before he made a million!

They stayed in. Meina rang her brother and apologised. Irena could not make on Sunday, besides, Meina was not sure if Chris will not be busy with Hashim on Sunday. So it was postponed for another day. She prepared the food. After dinner, Meina watched TV programme while Chris remained busy with his business plan. She was wondering why he couldn't do it during the day!

At night, Meina was in bed, she was reading a magazine while Chris was in the bathroom. Soon Chris came and laid beside her, 'sorry about earlier but you see it is very important for me.'

'I understand darling.' Meina did not wish to spoil the night. Chris had not been very active in bed for a while: either he was getting ready to go to Switzerland or phone to a number of estate agents and then to Hashim, he never had time. It had been a few weeks before they made proper love.

'Good,' he put his lamp off and got ready to sleep.

Meina also put her magazine away and turned the light off of her bedside the lamp. Soon they were kissing. Chris' hands moved to her breast and then on to her tummy. Meina was happy. But before they could get going, Chris stopped. He seemed very tired. He took off his hands from her body and lay quiet with his eyes closed. Meina tried to push the broken down vehicle but found she could not move it. Even her delicate hands could not revive the tired engine! After a few minutes, she realised that Chris had fallen asleep. She took her hands off his body and cursed all the selfish men in the world. She wondered how men with more than one wife managed! This bloke could not manage one! She stayed restless and frustrated for a while then she thought of Terry and Chuck. How masculine they were! God, they could make a woman happy with their hands alone! It wasn't long before she also fell asleep.

The next day, just after breakfast, Meina received a call from Sharon. She invited both of them to a casual dinner at her place; Meina excused stating that Chris was going to a business meeting. Sharon knew it anyway since Chris had already told her before. 'Why don't you come darling… what are you going to do alone at home?' She asked.
'Oh…I …I mean I was thinking to go to my mum.'
'Nonsense, mothers' day is Sunday…Saturday, it is time to enjoy with your friends! I mean with people of your own age!'
'I have just been to your place last week…it is your turn to come.'
'Sure, Terry and I would love to come but today you come.'
'Wouldn't I be in between you and Terry…I know Chuck is back in New York.' Meina lowered her voice.
'Not at all Meina, you know I am becoming more and more fond of you…otherwise, I am going to be bored…I had not planned anything for this Saturday.'
'I….'
Before Meina could say anything, 'please Meina…I want you to taste my new dish.' Sharon pleaded.

'Okay, baba…I will come, let me check with Chris.'

'Fine, I will see you.' Sharon was off the phone.

Meina went to the lounge where Chris was on his laptop. 'Is it alright if I go to Sharon, she had invited both of us to dinner?'

'You know I am busy tonight…I think it will be nice for you to get friendly with her; she is a very lively person.' Chris raised his head.

Meina was surprised, what a sudden change! The other day he had called her a bitch, and asked her to be careful of her. He did not know that she was already very friendly with her and Terry! She also did not know that Chris had his eye on Sharon! 'Okay, what sort of time will you be back?'

'I think we might go to casino after the meeting, Hashim likes the casino. I am going to be quite late, you can take the car, I will take a taxi besides, I might have a few drinks.'

'Alright then, but please don't over drink.'

'Sure.' Chris went back to his laptop.

The D Day arrived, Sharon was anxious everything to work. She put the hidden camera in the lounge and in the bedroom, and the remote unit in the spare bedroom. She was not sure which room they were likely to use? She also cooked an Austrian dish Wiener schnitzel and had bought some Austrian pastries from the special shop. White Austrian wine was to accompany the meal.

The evening arrived and Meina entered the house with a tin of Foie Gras, she had bought for the occasion, a favourite of Sharon who was dressed modestly, and Terry was also casual. 'Oh, I am so pleased to see you,' Sharon greeted her affectionately, kissing her on both of her cheeks. Terry was also happy, he always enjoyed her company.

Foie Gras was a good starter and lively conversation broke out. Wiener schnitzel was a success and Terry suggested that she cook it more often. Meina also loved it, while the Austrian wine went well with the food. 'What's the matter? I am not going to take advantage of you.' Terry asked Meina when she did not want her glass refilled.

'No, it is good but I think last time I got carried away with the champagne!' Meina suddenly remembered the excesses of the past week. 'Here, let me serve you this fine freshly squeezed orange juice.' Sharon offered her a new glass. The light crispy apple strudel with cream was a fine end to an enjoyable meal. 'You are such a good cook!' remarked Meina.

'Soon, you will know all my talents!' Sharon laughed.

After dinner, they moved to the lounge. Sharon put the new Adele album she had bought, and the room was filled with the beautiful voice of Adele. While they were listening to the fine music and chatting, suddenly, Sharon's mobile rang. 'Yes, Sharon speaking' Sharon answered the phone and with a gesture of hand she excused herself and moved to the hall. Soon Sharon was back 'I am afraid I will have to leave you guys for a short while.'

'What's the matter?' Terry asked hurriedly. He did not like the interruption to the pleasant evening they were having.

'Oh it is really nothing; Mrs Rowland, a customer has changed her plans; she is flying tomorrow early in the morning to Montreal. She is requesting if she can pick up her painting?'

'Why didn't she pick up in the day?' Terry's voice showed slight irritation.

'The picture came only this afternoon, after framing and special packaging for the journey; she was supposed to pick it up Monday morning but...let's leave the details out, I will be back before you realise that I had gone. I bet Adele will give you a good company.' Sharon looked at Meina.

'Let's go altogether' suggested Meina. She did not feel comfortable being alone with Terry.

'Yeah, it's a good idea.' Terry said.

'No, please do not spoil the evening…I won't be long …my Audi is
really fast; besides, there is only room for two in the car!' Sharon smiled.
'And I will make the coffee when I come back.'
Meina wanted to say something. 'Just sit tight my dear…Terry is going to
behave himself!' Sharon looked at both of them. She left the room, and
soon they heard the sound of Audi Sports car leaving the house.

Terry and Meina stayed quiet in the lounge listening to the music. After a
few minutes, Terry got up and changed the music, piano instrumental,
and turned the volume down. 'Is that alright?' Terry asked.
'That's fine, I love piano.' Meina replied.
'Can I get you some drink?'
'Perhaps, a drop of orange juice.'
Terry smiled; he got up, filled her glass with orange juice, and his glass
with Austrian wine. He brought the glass to her and sat in a sofa close to
her. 'Thanks.' Meina took the glass.
'To your health.' Terry raised his glass.
'And to yours.' Meina also raised her glass.

They were quiet for a few moments. 'Sharon takes her job seriously!'
Terry said.
'Yes these days, women have to be as competitive as men!'
'I agree…how is Chris? I heard he is into the property business. He
bought some paintings recently from Sharon for his properties.'
Meina did not know that Chris had met Sharon but she ignored it. 'Yes,
he couldn't find a suitable job.' Meina said softly. 'Why was he really
fired?' she asked.
'He must have told you that he was involved too much with this Middle
Eastern fellow…it affected his judgement.'
'He once said that you did not like him.'
'On the contrary, my dear, I really liked his work. I think he is a very
clever solicitor.'
'Maybe so, but he has been miserable at home and has been very
frustrated.'

'I hope he is okay with you' Terry looked into her eyes.

Meina is quiet; she felt comfortable talking to him. From last week, she was a little apprehensive that he will start from where they had left! How could she tell him that Chris has been terrible since he left the job, had not had sex with her for weeks, will not socialise. 'He has been visiting his mum in Switzerland, and often Hashim is in London and he spends time with him.' Meina complained.
'I don't know which fool would leave such a beautiful woman at home.' Terry sounded sympathetic. 'You know Meina, in life, we all need to make some adjustments; sometimes men and sometimes women have to sacrifice in order to save their marriages.'
'I know…God…I am trying hard!' Meina slipped.

In the spare bedroom, Sharon was waiting patiently after entering back home quietly. She had left the garden gate open to get back into the house without them noticing. They seemed to be talking like they were in an office; she regretted that she did not put a little Vodka in Meina's orange juice. She could not hear what they were talking.

In the lounge, after a few moments of quietness, Terry asked Meina if he could see her hand. Meina was surprised she did not know Terry was interested in palmistry. She moved and sat next to him on the sofa and put her hand forward. Terry takes her hand into his; suddenly, she felt the warmth of a man. 'I can see you have a long life.' Terry predicted.
'Everyone says that!' Meina smiled.
'No, this line is your life line…you see it is such a long line.' Terry put his finger on a line in her hand.
'Okay.'
'You are going to have four children.'
'How can you say that…I only want two children?'
'Well, I can't tell you all my trade secrets!' Terry smiled.
'Okay, let's move on.'
'You will be married twice.'
'What!?'

'Well, that's what it says!'

'Oh God...'

'Were you married before?'

'No Chris was my first boyfriend and he became my husband.' Meina's face showed anxiety.

'Don't worry; my dear, these grey hair (he did not have grey hair) get some times things wrong.' Terry tried to take the impact out.

'Okay, let's continue.'

'You are going to meet a slightly older man who is going to kiss you.'

'What....? Before Meina could finish, Terry kissed her lightly on her lips.

'Cheating! You took the fees before the work is completed!' Meina laughed. 'Okay, seriously let's continue.'

'I don't really know very much, it is just a hobby, not really developed...but I can tell you that what I see in your hand: a woman with warm heart who is emotional and very romantic!'

'You really think so?'

'No, these are your hand lines...look your hand is so warm.' Terry kissed her hand.

Meina looked into his eyes, how she could tell him, she has had no sex for weeks, and that a handsome man's touch has made her warm. Terry felt more confident she had not taken her hand away from his. He enjoyed touching the sexy woman. His experience with women told him that it was the right time to move. He put his hand on her shoulder and pulled her towards him and kissed her; this time, it was not a light kiss but a kiss which increased in intensity gradually. Meina was wondering what is happening! She was not drunk, she hardly had any drinks but she did not stop him! After couple of minutes, Meina felt Terry's hand on her breast, she tried to move his hand away but found that his other hand had moved to her lap. Meina did not move his hand and Terry felt the warmth of her body through the light material trouser she was wearing. He moved his hand slowly in between her thighs. After a few moments, Meina could not resist any longer. She left the caution behind, and pulled him towards her; her hands started massaging his back. Terry was far too experienced, he realised that the time was right. He knew that it will be about three quarter of an hour before Sharon will be back so there was no time to lose. Such a beautiful and sexy young woman, he could not believe his luck. He pushed her on the sofa and put his body on hers; this time, Meina did not move! His hands found her breast and massaged her nipples; Meina had not felt like that for a long time.

It wasn't long before Terry's hand moved inside her pants, Meina tried to stop him by trying to remove his hand but she knew, the way she stopped him, was putting more pressure on his hand, and it further excited Terry. Finally, Meina realised that the matter had gone too far, there was no turning back now. The young woman and not so young man helped each other taking their clothes off. Terry was amazed she really was a very pretty woman, very feminine, very hot and very sensuous! With passion they both looked at each other's bodies; they touched it, massaged it, tasted it and finally, Terry entered in her. He thought he was in heaven, the softness, the heat of the body and her perfume! Cadbury had never tasted so good! After a long time, Meina has had an orgasm. She enjoyed their love making as much, if not more.

Time passed quickly. Terry could spend the whole night with her. But Meina looked at her watch and realised that it was nearly an hour since Sharon had left. Terry was slightly massaging her body, and she knew that it won't be too long before they could start the exercise again. She gently moved his hand and got up. Terry looked at her naked body; he couldn't take his eyes off her. He was wondering who was prettier, Meina or Sharon? Meina definitely had an edge for being sexy, she was younger and she was really hot! Meina picked up her clothes and a couple of spoiled tissues from the floor and rushed towards the bathroom. Terry stayed for a few moments, thinking that Sharon could be back any time he also got up, picked up his clothes and started dressing.

In a few minutes, Meina came back to the lounge, fully dressed. She seemed shy; she looked a different person than a few minutes before. She sat down quickly on the sofa. Terry looked at her, excused himself and went also to the bathroom. Meina made sure that the sofa and the floor did not give anything away. She pushed the sofa slightly as it had moved

a little during their lovemaking. Terry came back shortly. He put back
Adele's album. 'Would you like something to drink?' Terry asked. 'Yes
please, a drop of cold wine.' Meina replied. Terry went to the kitchen and
brought two fresh glasses of wine. 'Here you are, my dear.' Terry offered
the glass to her.
'Thanks.' Meina took the glass without looking at him.
'I took a higher fee for seeing your hand...no?' Terry smiled.
Mina looked at him. 'No, it was my fault,' she said in a low voice.
Terry got up from his chair and came to her and kissed on her hair lightly.
'You are a beautiful woman, I tell you Chris is really lucky to have you
as his wife, there was no fault; nothing happened,' he looked into her
eyes meaningfully. He went back to his seat.

It wasn't long before they heard the house door opening and Sharon
walked into the lounge. 'God, you guys are still sitting at the same place
where I left you!' she exclaimed. 'I see, at least, Terry has served you a
decent drink!'

Meina smiled, Terry stayed quiet.

Meina arrived home and found Chris was not yet back. She felt guilty for
what she had done. She had never been unfaithful to her husband. She
went to the bathroom. While she was taking bath she looked at herself,
she never realised that she was so sexy. Not many people called her very
beautiful in the office but often she will have to dampen the spirit of
some colleagues who always thought that she was very sexy, and trying
different ways to touch her. She felt her body, smooth skin, firm breast,
shapely legs, she wasn't bad at all, she thought. But soon when she
realised what she had done, she started crying 'you have been stupid' she
said to herself. Then she thought about Terry. God! What a charming
man, handsome, rich and bloody clever. How he seduced her by reading

her hand, as though, I did not know that it was the way to start touching me, but why I did not stop him! I cannot blame alcohol; I was perfectly in my senses. I wish Chris would learn a few things from Terry who knew perfectly well how to satisfy a woman. It was Sharon who really was lucky, she concluded.

A few minutes later, she heard the flat door opening. 'Meina,' she heard Chris from lounge.
'I am in the bath,' replied Meina. Chris who was drunk moved to the bedroom from the lounge and started changing his clothes. He did not bother to come to the bathroom. 'God…what a prick he has become, couldn't he come to the bathroom and see me in the bath and then we could…,' she thought.
By the time Meina went to the bedroom Chris had fallen asleep. He had too much to drink, and had lost all the winnings in the end at the casino; Hashim had lost a lot more. Meina went to the bed quietly. She didn't think that Chris would have liked to be woken up or was able to do anything! She fell asleep.

Monday was as hectic as it should be, Terry was in the office, Chris was looking some property details, Sharon busy at the gallery, and Meina was in her office. About mid-day, Terry's secretary informed him that Mr Norman Betts, the new CFO of Green Park International was there. 'Please ask Peter to join me in my office' Terry went outside and received Norman and brought him to his office. Soon Peter Cooper joined them. 'How is Wolfie?' asked Terry.
'He is fine. Sorry, he couldn't make it; he was meeting one of the investors for lunch.' Norman replied.
'How are you getting along?'
'I am finding my feet, the finance team is really competent… my job is to get ready for the IPO.'
'Have you seen some of the reports?' asked Peter.

'Yes, most of these, so I am reasonably familiar what's going on.'
'Good.' Terry said.
'Where is Chuck? I haven't met him,' asked Norman.
'He is in our New York office; he should be here in a few days,' replied Peter.
'I see... what concerns me ...' Norman looked around and hesitated.
'Please do not worry, nothing goes out of this office until I okay it, so you can speak freely. We also do periodic scan for any bugs!' Terry assured Norman; while Peter was surprised to hear about scanning.
'I think you guys have been looking some funds transfers from the US...these transactions were done a few years ago...I do not think we should be spending our time on it!'
'I understand,' Terry replied, 'I know Chuck had looked at some of the transactions and looked at its movement.'
'Yes, I have seen some notes from Mark (FC), he mentioned Chuck has been spending a lot of time on it.' Norman did not clarify his concern.
'Yes, I was working on some of these transfers with Chuck.' Peter added.

Terry knew exactly where Norman was coming from; he also understood why Norman did not have a meeting at Green Park's office. 'I think Chuck was looking at these in connection with FCA investigation, but now the investigation is over, there is no reason to continue looking at these old transactions; maybe he was just tying up loose ends.'
'Well, one can look at these, if needed in future; all records are there, as you know the company's policy is to keep the records a lot longer than required by statute.' Norman justified his argument.
'I will ask Chuck not to look anything which is not very relevant, I also understand that you want to concentrate on the IPO... we are here to help you as and when you need it.' Terry did his PR.
'Great, I think you understand.' Norman looked at Terry and Peter.
They continued to discuss for a while, and left for lunch in a nearby restaurant where the table was already booked for them.

Chapter 12

After a few days, Chris was in his flat looking at the post. Meina had left for her office. He was dressed casually in the lounge and started opening the post which normally came after when they had gone to their offices. Since he was currently working from home, he opened the post. Usual bills, property details from estate agents, and then suddenly, he noticed some photographs in an envelope. Chris nearly fainted when he saw the photographs. These showed Meina and Terry; he could not recognise where they were but it seemed the lounge or room of a home, and it was not of his flat. When he looked at some more photos, it seemed that these were Sharon's home. Chris looked at the photographs again. One showed Meina and Terry kissing then progressively both of them naked, touching each other and then what he could not bear to see, Terry inside Meina's mouth and inside…… These were very explicit and clear photos.

He could not believe, the fucking bitch how she hated in her mouth but with Terry she seemed to be enjoying it. He went into rage and picked up the calculator and threw it on the photograph of him with Meina on the wall. The calculator did not catch the frame but broke with impact on the wall. 'Meina, how could you…,' he almost spoke as he thought. He put the photos down on the table and put his hands on his head, eyes closed. He could see the photos inside his mind, Meina and Terry together. Even, the photographs from the table seemed to be staring at him, and laughing at him. His face went pale. He never thought in his life that he will ever see such a thing; she has been his girlfriend since college days, and then became his wife.

Chris did not know how long he sat there on the chair with his eyes closed. Then he opened his eyes and took the photographs in his hand to ensure he was not dreaming. Normally, whenever he thought of Meina, her smiling face used to come in front of him but not now, all he could see she was laying under Terry and...... 'Why Meina...why?' he shouted. But she was far away from him. He started walking in the lounge forward and backward; his fists clenched, the face instead of pale, blood red.

It was nearly an hour before he calmed down. He went to the kitchen and drank cold water, plenty to cool him down. He felt a little better, came back to the lounge. He took the photographs again and looked at them. He put the radio on and heard the melodic voice of an artist singing:

"I feel nothing, I do nothing, I expect nothing without you.
I have nothing, my life is nothing, it is just void without you.
I am nothing without you, yes my man..."   © May 2015

The song did not help. Only word which came to his mind was 'fucking liar' he put the radio off.

Chris went to the drink cupboard in the lounge and poured some scotch for him. After taking a few large sips, he felt a little better; the bitter scotch fought with his bitter mood but could not win. He took the photographs again. He saw Terry's face, 'look at that bastard, how is he lusting after someone else's wife!! 'Shit, shit, shit,' he said to himself. He felt like going to Henry Sheldon's offices and smash Terry's face. After a few moments, hitting Terry in his mind several times, he cooled down, 'is it my fault? Have I neglected my wife? Can't they do without sex for a short while?' he knew he had neglected her in the past few weeks. It seemed Terry was taunting him. 'Hey buddy, you wanted to fuck Sharon and look ... I have already fucked your wife!' God, how it is terrible, bloody whores cannot keep their legs closed! He continued to fume and kept insulting Terry and all women. He turned his laptop off, threw the mail including one or two envelopes unopened to the floor, and started drinking. When he noticed his glass was empty, he brought the bottle of scotch from the cupboard, and sat in the lounge drinking scotch.

After a large quantity of scotch in his tummy, and few hours later, it was nearly lunch time but Chris was not hungry. He went to the kitchen picked up a packet of crisp from the cupboard and came back in the lounge. He ate the crisps and started drinking the malt whiskey again on almost empty stomach. He felt drunk, threw the photographs at the floor and went to the bedroom. He slept, not quite sure how long for? He had been having late nights, and had been travelling recently.

In the evening, Meina got back from her office. Throughout the journey on the tube, she was thinking, she was going to make up with Chris; she had no right to be so indiscrete. He was upset and too busy to start a new career in the property and running around to get his self-esteem back. She knew many women in India stayed without their husbands for months while their husbands worked in the USA, UK and Middle East. If everyone was like her?!! She felt ashamed. She also decided to distance a little from Sharon. She was going to be a model wife, she resolved.

When she arrived at the flat, she opened the door, there was no light; she thought Chris was not a home. Then she went to the lounge and saw the post lying around including some photos, there was also broken a calculator. She smiled; Chris was having his frustrations out on the calculator…until she picked up one photo. Now it was Meina's turn to almost faint, the shock was too much! She controlled herself and picked up other photos and looked at them, yes it was hers. She recognised the place, it was Sharon's home.

She sat down still in shock. Then she got up after a few moments, and without feeling any energy in her body she tidied up the lounge: she put the post in order, collected all the photos and opened the unopened envelopes. She looked at the photos again; who could do such a thing!

The graphic details in a few photos, she felt like burning them straight away. Somehow, she took the envelope and put the photos back inside it and sat down.

She was still not sure where Chris was? She did not have the courage to face him. With remorse and anger, she was overwhelmed, she started crying. After a few minutes, she wiped her face with her handkerchief, hid the photos in her hand bag and went to the bedroom. The room was dark; on the chair, Chris was sitting with blank face. He put her handbag and came near Chris. 'Hi darling,' she wanted to kiss him. He stopped her with his hand without speaking. He did not look at her. She took her jeans and went to the bathroom to change. There she looked at herself. All the glow at her face was gone, she saw a miserable, worried face; it certainly did not look like the photo of the woman in the photograph. She refreshed herself and changed into jeans and decided to be a little more courageous. She went to the bedroom; Chris was still sitting in the dark looking passively on the floor.

Meina put the light on; Chris still did not notice her. She tried remembering the psychology she had studied at the university but they never taught how to deal with a man who suddenly learnt that his beloved wife was screwing, especially with people who though not his enemy, but who had fired him from his job. She dreaded the worst. With courage, she came close to him and sat down on the bed near his chair. 'Chris I am really sorry, please let me explain,' she pleaded.

Chris looked at her, Meina would always remember those eyes; it looked like the eyes of a wounded wolf. She was frightened; she had never seen him like that before. 'Okay, explain.' Chris said icily.
'I think someone has played a trick; these photos are fabrication.' Meina tried to lie.
'Don't fucking make a fool of me.' Chris barked. At the same time, he slapped her hard on her face. Her lip was cut and few drops of blood came from it. Meina, without making any sound, took a tissue from the side table and cleaned her lips.

'Chris, I promise you these are not what it looks.' Meina continued with her lies.

'You stupid bitch… what are you talking about! No one can fabricate these pictures.' Chris exploded again, but this time, he did not raise his hand. He looked at her but could not see his beloved wife but a woman who not only cheated him but now lying to make a fool of him. 'You have been fucking all that time with Terry, haven't you?'

Meina was quiet; she knew that there was no point in lying any more. 'I swear to you I only slept with him once, and that was only last week but it did not happen the way these photos show.' Meina had tears in her eyes.

'Thank you for admitting, I would have gone and broken that son of a bitch's face, I had to really control myself,' he snorted.

Meina was quiet; her tears were now flowing from her eyes. Seeing her cry cooled him a little bit, women's tears always do! 'Meina, you have disappointed me to the degree I cannot explain, how could you?' his voice, a mixture of anger and bitter disappointment.

'I was lonely; you have not paid much attention to me in the last few weeks. I got drunk….' Meina did not really know what to say.

'I have been fired, I have been unsuccessful in finding a job; then I try to set up a new business. I have been rushing like mad everywhere, sorry if I neglected you.' Chris was sarcastic.

Meina looked at the floor, and after collecting a little courage, 'I felt you did not like me anymore.'

'Don't be so fucking stupid, woman; just because I did not… wait…yes I did not fuck you for a few weeks, you had to go and fuck with that bastard,' he shouted in gutter language.

'Look instead of hitting me or screaming like a lunatic, let's talk like adults.' Meina mustered her courage.

'Yes...of course I am a lunatic, I forgot to sleep with my wife due to my career problems, so she had to go and satisfy herself outside.' Chris shouted with anger and sarcasm.

Meina did not reply, suddenly Chris got up. 'Alright, I am going to satisfy your desires.' He pushed her on the bed where she was sitting and almost tore her blouse, then he undid her jeans; Meina was not quite sure if she should stop him or let him continue. Before she could make up her mind, she found herself naked on the bed. 'Don't be silly Chris, wait...let's have dinner...' Meina did not finish her sentence; she noticed he had taken his clothes off. 'Alright tell me where that bastard has not been?' He slapped on her face again and sat on her. Meina tried to push him away but he was far too strong. Then he brought his penis near her mouth, 'alright... but no... Terry has already been here, you fucking slut...' then he went in between her thighs 'alright... but no...Terry also has been here; perhaps too many times!' Meina could not bear to look at him.

Suddenly, Chris with his hands turned her over, now she was facing the bed while he was still sitting on top of her. Meina tried to move but his strong hands and body held her. 'Yes of course, this is the place where Terry did not enter, or did he?' He spread her legs apart and lifted her bottom a little by putting his hand under her tummy, and then with a thrust, he entered in her back. 'Ooh...ooh...' Meina shrieked. She felt a horse has entered in her back, the pain was too much. 'Chris please....no...it's really painful!' she cried with pain. She tried last time to push him away, but she could not. Chris was almost in trance, he ignored her pleas. For couple of minutes, she continued to scream while Chris inflicted on her the pain she had not known before. However, the ordeal was quickly over. He climaxed in couple of minutes or so, but for Meina, it was probably the longest two minutes of her life.

After lying next to her in the bed for a few minutes, while Meina continued to cry, and feeling humiliated, Chris got up without looking at her. He put his clothes on and went to the spare bedroom collecting his scotch bottle from the lounge on the way. The man was still in his trance!

Meina and Chris did not have any dinner that night, they did not speak to each other. After a while, Meina got up from the bed. She noticed a few drops of blood on the bed sheet, her bottom was still painful. It seems something was burning inside her. Seeing the blood on the sheet made her even more disgusted. She went to the attached bathroom and took a shower. She cleaned her lips and put some lotion on the cut, then she examined her bottom in the mirror, there was no apparent damage in her back.

After the shower, she put her nightie and changed the bed sheet. She put the light off and lay on the bed. She started thinking why such a lovely man would behave in such a disgusting and crude way. She did not mind when he slapped her, but his raping in her back was intolerable. How could he….? She felt tears again in her eyes. She did not have such a pain when she had lost her virginity, and to whom….the same disgusting person who had just violated her, she started crying again.

After about half an hour, she cooled down; the flow of tears and the punishment had taken her guilt away. Who sent those photos? Who took them? Why, why… she started thinking. In the other bedroom, a well-educated qualified solicitor did not ask himself the same questions; he even got drunk. Meina tried to analyse, is it Sharon? But why, somehow she knew that we were going to sleep and she was jealous but in the past, she had encouraged her to be free with her husband, she claimed it had affected him positively, and resulted in a better performance in the bedroom! In fact, once she thought even Sharon wanted to sleep with her! I am a woman too but I couldn't read her mind even though, I am a qualified with psychology degree. She got up and drank some water which was kept in a jug on the sideboard.

She pressed her mind hard. Was it Terry? But he was too busy with her, maybe a hidden camera triggered when he was busy with her. Sharon had gone to her gallery, she had heard her car and heard her again when she came back. But what Terry had to gain? He himself had to lose as much as her if these photos were shown to Sharon or indeed to his office. Chuck was in New York but then he is such a lovely person. She decided she needed to work it out more next day. Now, how she was going to deal with the current situation? She felt Chris was still at home in the spare bedroom. She got up and put the bolt on the door. She continued to think while her bottom was still painful. Time passed and she fell asleep. Her husband did the same in the other room, without changing his clothes.

Next morning, Meina rang her office stating that she was sick. Chris was still sleeping in the spare bedroom. Terry was in his office busy as usual in his daily activities, he had no idea what Meina went through. Sharon was in the gallery; she had brought her new 'toy' to the gallery and installed it in the office with a camera to the front of display room. Now she could take pictures of any visiting person without resorting to the CCTV. She had almost forgotten what she had done. However, she wanted to learn what was Chris reaction to the photos? She decided to call Meina at her mobile. Meina excused herself stating that she was not well and would call her back. Meina did not notice any change in Sharon, or noticing any guilt in her voice, she was as lively as ever.

Meina started packing up her essential clothes in a suitcase; put all the necessary papers and her jewellery. She checked the disgusting photos in her hand bag. She looked more like a porn star rather than an HR officer. Meina took the photos to the kitchen and cremated them. The erotic photographs became ashes in a minute. She felt a little better after burning it. She put the ashes into the sink and the cold water took the photos and its 'dirt' with it in the gutter where they belonged.

She came back to the bedroom and looked around as though she was seeing it last time. She suddenly remembered what had happened last night, and it sent waves of anger and disgust all over her body. She heard the opening of the door of the spare bedroom; Chris was going to the common bathroom. She waited till she heard the door closing. She put her shoes, took the small suitcase and her handbag, and left the flat quietly. Quickly, she left the building and even did not hear 'Good morning Mrs Sneale,' from the concierge. She took a taxi and went to her mum's house.

Chris, while in the bathroom, heard the front door opening and closing. He knew it was Meina going to the office, quite late though! He had a severe headache, the large quantity of scotch on empty stomach, the night before, showed its result now, He took the shower and then went to the main bedroom. He dressed himself and then went to the kitchen. He did not notice anything unusual in the bedroom. The kitchen was also neat; it seemed no plate had been touched. He took a large bowl of cereal with cold fresh milk and sat down on the breakfast table. The cold milk and cereal made his tummy a little better; then he made some tea. He began to feel better but the headache had not gone. He took a couple of paracetamol tablets from the drawer and swallowed it with his tea.

A few minutes later, he came to the lounge, his yesterday's post was arranged on the table neatly, and his laptop was there too. He looked at the papers but did not find the photographs. Of course, Meina had put them away not to annoy him any further, he thought. Suddenly, he recalled his behaviour the evening before. He could not believe the way he had behaved. 'Shit man, you have over done it!!' he said to himself. Then he remembered the photographs and the graphic details, and his face became tense again, his fists clenched. It took him a few minutes to cool down again.

He started to analyse the situation just like Meina, who took the photographs? Who sent them and who was to gain out of it? His legal brain started working but headache and his mental position was not quite up to it. He excluded Chuck since he knew that he was in New York, from the conversation with Meina when they had planned their different engagements for Saturday evening. It could not have been Terry; he had as much, if not more to lose. In fact, he could use those photos to get at him, he thought. Someone wanted to hurt him or Meina. Surely Sharon could not have; who in their right mind would let their husbands sleep with their friends! Maybe she did! A revenge for the loss of her lover, Lenny who was fired from the office basically due to him. But did he ask

Lenny to fuck with his boss's wife!? Fool! The photographs looked professional; it looked like someone was actually posing for it. No Sharon would have been as hurt as he was with that. Little he knew of a woman's mind!!

Chris tried to look for the photographs in the lounge. After not finding it there, he went to the bedroom and opened the side board drawers, and then he opened Meina's wardrobe. He checked in the small drawer in the wardrobe where she kept some of her private papers and jewellery etc. There was nothing. In fact, her jewellery was not there either. Then he noticed the empty hangers in the wardrobe, a number of empty hangers, now he realised that Meina had left the house! It was time for another shock for him, even though, not as acute as yesterday. He was still angry with her. He decided that it was important to settle his score with Hamiltons; he needed to fuck that bitch as soon as possible. He rang Sharon. 'Hey… how are you Chris?' Sharon replied in her usual way. 'I am okay, I was wondering if we could meet for a lunch or maybe for a drink after your work.'
'Sorry Chris, not for couple of days, but I will ring you soon. Are you going to buy some more pictures?'
'Not at the moment, but in due course. Can I count on you to ring me?'
'Of course Chris, I want both of you to be our family friends.' Sharon replied in her seductive voice.
'Sure, same here.'
'Bye.'
'Bye.'

When Meina arrived at home, her brother had already gone to the pharmacy. Her mum opened the door and was surprised to see her unexpectedly.

'Hi mumiji.'

'Hello beta, what a pleasant surprise!' Then Leena noticed the suitcase, 'I
see you are going to stay for a few days.' She seemed happy to see her
daughter.

'No mum, perhaps a little longer!' They both entered into the house.

'Let me make a cup of tea for you.' Leena noticed her charming
daughter's lip was cut and her face very pale.

Meina went upstairs in her bedroom where she used to live prior to the
wedding, and her mother had kept it as it was. Sometimes, she stayed
there in the evening or weekend. After putting the clothes in the
wardrobe, she came down to the kitchen where on the breakfast table,
Leena was waiting for her.

'What's the matter darling, you look pale!' Leena dreaded that she had a
row with Chris.

'In a minute Mumiji; let me have some tea, I have not had anything since
yesterday lunch time.' Meina picked the tea cup.

'Oh my poor darling! Let me make breakfast for you.'

'No mumiji, I am not hungry.' Meina took a sip, but before another sip,
she broke down. She started crying loudly. Leena got up from her chair
and rushed towards her daughter and put her arms around her. She kissed
on her hair. 'My darling, don't cry, your mum is here…what's the
matter?' Meina continued to cry. After a few moments, 'it's Chris,
mumiji, he has been terrible!'

'What happened?'

Meina stopped crying, picked up a tissue and cleaned her eyes and nose.
She explained to her mum the version as she saw it. She told her that she
had been neglected for a long time, she tried to put up with it, Chris will
disappear in Switzerland often, and in London, he spent a lot of time with
his new friend Hashim, and that she slept with a friend's husband. Chris
learnt about it and beat her up. Leena was horrified when she learnt that
her daughter has been unfaithful. 'You shouldn't have, my darling; this is
not the way our women behave!' Leena expressed her view. 'But on the
same token, he shouldn't have raised his hand on you…I can see your
lips cut!' she sat next to her.

'That is not all mum, he raped me!' Meina showed her anger.

'Now come on my darling, husbands do not rape their wives! They have the fucking right to sleep with their wives.' Leena remembered the past experience and the stories of other women.
'You don't mean that literally, do you!... even they do not have the right to sleep with their wives without their consent.'
'The consent is implied when you get married.' Leena insisted.
'Wait till I tell you where he raped me, it was in my bottom!' Meina put her eyes on the floor when she said it, she felt embarrassed to even tell her mum. Chris had never before shown any inclination towards sodomy. Leena was shocked. 'That is bad... he shouldn't have done that,' her face showed first time sign of unpleasantness. They both were quiet for a while.
'Tell me Meina, how Chris knew about your indiscretion? Did he see you, were you in your flat and caught unguarded?'
'No mumiji, I was visiting one of my best friends Sharon, I had drunk a bit of wine, she had to go somewhere for an hour or so, I was with her husband alone ...I got carried away. He seduced me; I just could not stop him. A few days later, some disgusting photographs arrived in the post to Chris (Meina did not want to admit to her mum that she did it in full sense and that she was not drunk at all)'.
'But who will send those photographs and who took them?' asked Leena.
'It is a mystery, maybe Chris suspected something and planned it that way or some enemy of Hamiltons or ours.'
'Do they get along alright?'
'Who...you mean Sharon and Terry...they really are very broad minded and very much in love, I never had the slightest hint of anything between them.'
'I don't know what to say...do you want me to call Balak?' Leena was as lost as her daughter.
'No mumiji, I am going to be here for a while, let's wait till evening...I want to just relax. Yesterday, it has been too much for me.'
Leena went into deep thoughts while Meina went upstairs in her bedroom.

In the evening, Sharon and Terry were sitting in the lounge. Terry was watching news on TV while Sharon was thinking. Why didn't Meina call her back, why did she sound so upset on the phone? Why Chris rang? She was dreading that her scheme does not misfire. 'Are you okay?' asked Terry when he saw her deep in thoughts.

'Yeah, I am fine, how was your office?'

'Everything seems to be okay, we have hired two bright new solicitors to replace Lenny and Chris....come to think of it, we need to invite them at our place soon.'

'I will arrange something.' Sharon said. To hear the name of Lenny, she had a strange feeling, she remembered him: smart, young and very handsome, and how he made her happy. To remember Lenny made her less worried about Meina and Chris. She really missed him. She also did not feel any guilt about her affair with him now, since she saw how Terry was behaving, as though nothing had happened between him and Meina. Men are hypocrite, she thought. Terry did not have the slightest guilt. Terry thought Sharon had no idea about his indiscretion.

The same evening, Chris was alone in his flat, he had rung Meina's office and had learnt that she had called sick. He felt embarrassed when they learnt, it was her husband. Somehow, he knew that she was not going to come back to him that evening. Has she really left him!!?

He could not wait any longer. He rang his mother in law.

'Hi Chris, how are you?' Leena asked in her usual way.

'I am alright mumiji...I and Meina had a row yesterday.'

'I know beta (son), she is here; shall I call her?'

'No thanks, just wanted to know where she was...she did not tell me anything!' He hung up.

He was not any more in his trance but still angry.

Chapter 13

About a month passed. Chris did not try to ask Meina back. He never forgave her; adding insult to injury, leaving the house without even telling him! He became erratic in his behaviour; Sharon met him once for a drink but turned his advances down, and made him know, in no uncertain terms, that she was never going to be one of his scores. Chris finally, waited for Meina to make a move. Leena and Balak tried to persuade Meina, to at least, meet Chris and see if there was any way forward, and they could start a new chapter. But Meina also did not forgive Chris. They both were still angry with each other, and no one was willing to forgive or forget what had happened.

Sharon invited Meina many times to her place but she declined. Sharon had learnt that Chris and Meina had separated. Chuck made another trip to the UK; Terry had reduced his involvement in Green Park International. Besides, Chuck had already finished his secret due diligence on Henry Sheldon LLP, and was going to give his final report to Sandy Gorfield.

One morning, Meina received a call from Chuck in her office. He wanted to meet her for lunch. 'I am sorry I am busy during lunch time but if you like we can meet after work.' Chuck jumped at the opportunity. 'Of course, that will be even better.'

They met in the City, and after a light drink, went to the West End for a meal. During the meal, they were talking, 'Sorry to be personal…but why did you split with Chris?' Chuck asked.

'He was my first serious boyfriend and we got married, I hardly knew any other men. He treated me as though I was dependent upon him.'
Meina became slightly sad remembering Chris but did not show.
'I know, Meina, in life, there are many ups and downs. Can I be of assistance, do you want me to talk to Chris?'
'No please, don't; he has not made any efforts to reconcile. If he wanted to call me or meet, he could have done.'
'May be, he is expecting you to start, some men are so chauvinistic pigs, just like me!'
'No I don't think he loves me anymore, I don't feel much for him either.'
'That's sad.'

They continued to talk. They finished their meals; Meina did not want to stay late. 'Can I invite you to my place for a drink or coffee, it's not late?' Chuck asked her.
'Sorry Chuck, not tonight...I made an effort to meet you. I have not been feeling very well recently...that is in my mind; sometimes, I feel really depressed.'
'Oh my dear, you need to look after yourself, I won't insist but at least, allow me to escort you to your home.'
Meina suddenly laughed, that was the first time in the whole evening. Chuck saw the old glimpse of Meina, 'I am not a little girl anymore!' she said.
'Of course not, but I will have some more time with you, I wish I could make you happy as you used to be.'
Meina looked at Chuck; first time, she felt the tenderness in his voice.
'Alright, I am going to take a taxi.'
'Fine,' Chuck looked around and after a few moments, stopped one passing black cab. They sat together in the taxi, Meina felt good ...it was the best she had felt since the split from Chris. They continued to talk. They both learnt a little more that evening about each other: their likings, hobbies and past times. Meina was relieved that Chuck did not try to touch her or get any physical. She felt quite relaxed spending some time with him.

The time passed quickly; soon they were at Meina's family home in Wimbledon. Both got out, Chuck made a sign to the driver to wait. Meina although would have been happy to spend some more time with him, did not feel like introducing him to her family yet. 'You will forgive me, if I do not ask you in.' Meina said in apologetic manner.

'Nonsense, I want you to feel absolutely comfortable with me.' Chuck took her hand in his. 'Meina, I want you to know that I am your friend and will always be.' Chuck said; his voice full of care and tenderness. Meina kissed him on his cheeks 'I am your friend too.'

'Alright, I will talk to you.' Chuck felt it was time to go.

'Bye Chuck, and thanks for a wonderful evening.'

'My pleasure mam, see you.' Chuck smiled and opened the door of the cab and sat down. Meina waved her hand and walked towards the house while Chuck gave the driver his hotel's name.

Leena, who had heard the car, saw them from the window discretely. It was the first time she had seen Chuck. She was pleased the way they had said goodbye to each other, without any long kisses or close hugging. She knew her daughter knew how to handle herself.

After days of persuasion from Leena, Balak and Irena, Meina accepted to meet Chris at her family home. Balak who did not know the full story except that they had an argument, was not very happy when he noticed her lips which Meina lied that it had nothing to do with Chris, and that she had fallen. Balak did not quite buy it but did not insist. He would not agree to the meeting, had he known that his sister was beaten and raped. He probably would have fought with Chris, had he known the manner in which she was raped! 'Beta, in our tradition, we need to make sure that our house is not broken. We cannot let them break their home; we are the girl's family, we have to play low!' Leena had advised her son. Looking back, she had not liked the idea that her daughter should be married to other than Indian origin person, but eventually, had learnt to like Chris. Since their marriage, she had always treated him like her own son.

Chris arrived promptly in the evening. Meina was back from the office. Balak came early from his pharmacy and Irena also joined them. They were all in the lounge except Meina. Leena had served them a nice Burgundy white wine. White wine had effect of cooling people down while red, she thought, reds were hot and made you excite too quickly. In a few minutes, Meina arrived. The idea was to make Chris comfortable before they both met. Chris got up and kissed her on her cheek lightly and sat down. Leena was pleased with his move. She had made a lot of efforts to please Chris: made the food he liked, his favourite wine and dessert, the kheer (an Indian rice pudding) which Chris adored.

Chris praised Leena's cooking, Irena drank a lot of wine; she was still getting used to hot Indian food. After the dinner, while Leena went into the kitchen, Balak got up. 'Sorry Chris, I need to drop Irena at her place, she has to attend the shooting in the morning; her company is preparing an advertisement on the TV and she needs to be there along with the producer and the models etc. I should be back in about an hour; see you later.' In a few moments, Leena also came from the kitchen; she looked at Meina and Chris who were now alone in the lounge. 'I am going to watch some TV in my room, if you need me please call.' Before they could say anything, she left the lounge.

After a few moments' quietness, Chris broke the silence, 'you did not even tell me that you were leaving home!' he complained.
'Sorry Chris, but in the circumstance, I would say that I had the courage to stay there overnight, I felt I should have left straight away,' Meina replied.
'I agree, I got carried away but those photos were really awful, I felt sick!'
'There is a limit to what one can do or what one can tolerate!' it was Meina's turn to complain.

'What do you mean?'

'I mean, it was too difficult for you to tolerate those filthy photos, I understand, but on the same token, I was able to put up with your slaps… but not with what followed!'

Chris was quiet for a few moments, trying to remember that awful night, Meina was expecting that he will apologise profoundly and beg for her forgiveness; even his facial expressions did not show anything. 'Look Chris (she did not use the usual word 'darling') you never called after, you never made any effort… it has been quiet for a few weeks, you could have called me and tried to find out how I was etc etc.'

'You could have done the same.' Chris argued.

Meina kept quiet and started thinking; there was an awkward silence while both of them looked at different things quietly without looking at each other. Finally, Meina broke the silence this time. 'Chris, I do not feel any love for you anymore,' she whispered without looking at him.

Chris looked at her in disbelief; he was not expecting that statement. He wondered why to go all that trouble to tell me that! He was expecting that she would fall on his feet, apologise for her adultery then he will also apologise for his rude behaviour. Meina felt it took hours before he spoke, 'Meina instead of apologising for fucking with my ex-boss who fired me, you are telling me that you do not feel any love for me…you are bloody amazing!!' Chris exploded even though, he kept the volume down.

'Look Chris, we are not children, we are not here to analyse our lives…I am sure I have not been a good wife to you!'

'I can feel the sarcasm in your voice?' Chris said angrily.

'Please forgive me, it was not intended.' The room fell into uncomfortable silence again.

'My mother who still believes in old Indian traditions, and to a certain degree, my brother, persuaded me to have this meeting…we are grown up and educated people, we do not need to fight; let's deal with it in a mature way.'

'Meina, I really don't understand why you guys invited me!?'

'I know, it was the last attempt. You see we both have gone our ways, I do not see any love in your eyes…you do not see any love or magic in mine…so let's behave as though nothing has happened, and go our separate ways.' Meina mustered courage but continued to look at the carpet.

Chris is disappointed; it showed on his face. He realised that he had lost his college girlfriend, the 'tight arse', 'snob' as his friends used to refer her. He got up from his chair and came close to her. 'Look at me Meina…I am your ex-boyfriend, your lover, your husband; are you sure that's what you want!?'

Meina did not look at him. 'You were all that to me and a lot more, a few months ago, but now I am sorry, you are almost a stranger to me!'

Chris is shocked; he goes back to his chair. Meina still did not look at him, her eyes remained fixed on the floor. 'Alright Meina, I understand, I will try to wind up this unfortunate union without causing any further heartache to you.' Chris got up and came to her. He kissed on her head gently. 'Please thank your mum for a very nice dinner.' Chris moved towards the door and opened it. Meina also got up, her eyes full of tears; she walked with him towards the main door. 'Goodbye Chris, I wish you all the best.' Meina whispered in a trembling voice.

'Goodbye Meina, same from me.' Chris moved out of the main door to his parked car in the driveway. Soon the car moved with a speed, Chris did not look at Meina who was standing at the main door looking at his car, her arm almost half way, waving him.

From the window, Leena noticed Chris leaving in the car with a speed, she feared the worst. It was soon confirmed by Meina's loud crying while she was rushing to her bedroom. Leena also started crying, her eyes full of tears, she realised that her efforts had failed.

Nearly four weeks passed. Sandy Gorfield invited Sir Henry Sheldon to New York with a view to discussing his firm possibly buying out Henry Sheldon LLP. Sir Henry pretended to be surprised in the meeting. He promised to consider it. The next stage would be for Sandy to visit London prior to formal discussion. They both appreciated Chuck's work in London. Terry's position became even more solid, he was de-facto number two in the practice. Terry threw a big party in which a number of his colleagues were invited. Chuck came especially from New York to attend it. Meina also attended the party having refused many times Sharon's invitation. Finally, she realised that it was time to move on.

It was Saturday, and at London Heathrow airport, terminal four, British Airways flight was getting ready for New York. Close to the main departure gate, there was an unusually large group of people. Meina and Chuck were going to New York. Terry and Sharon were there to see them off along with Meina's family.

'I wish you all the best for future,' Sharon hugged Meina warmly. 'I never wanted to hurt you Meina,' she whispered in Meina's ears. Meina looked at her, not quite understanding but touched by her warm hug and tenderness in her voice. She also appreciated that Hamiltons came to see her off. While Sharon was kissing Meina, Terry came close to her and also hugged her but lightly. 'Sharon and I are your friends for ever. Whenever you visit London please remember us.' 'Thank you Terry.' Meina's voice was stuck in her throat, all kinds of emotions engulfing her. She was going to settle down in New York. Sharon hugged Chuck and whispered 'Thanks Chuck, really appreciate…..' Terry shook hand with him.

Then it was Irena who hugged her, 'take care Meina, all the best.' 'Thanks Irena, I hope to see you soon, maybe with some good news (her expected engagement with Balak)!' Balak was really sad, he loved his only sister. He knew from New York, she will not be able to come frequently. He also hugged her close and kissed on her cheeks. 'Balak is always there for you, my darling sister,' he was almost in tears. Then he shook hands with Chuck, 'please take care of my sister.' Chuck saw his tears; he put his other hand on Balak's hand and squeezed it, 'just like my life!' Finally, it was Leena she was standing there and crying. She hugged her daughter close. 'Don't forget your mumiji,' she said it as she kissed her cheeks. 'My darling; be more patient with men,' she whispered slowly in her ears. Meina started crying, 'mum…' she could not say any more. Then Leena hugged Chuck. 'May God be with you, and you have a very happy and contented life.'

'Thank you, mumiji.' Chuck had learnt the Indian way of addressing her. 'I will take care of your daughter,' he reassured Leena.

Not far from the terminal four, there was another flight; Emirates Airline was almost ready to take off for the Gulf. Inside the plane, in the business class, there was a passenger who came in a taxi to the airport because his mum lived in Switzerland and his dad, who lived in Bristol, could not come to London. None of his friends came to see him off. Chris looked sad, and looked at the newspaper without any real interest. He was offered a job in the Gulf, by Hashim, and he was going to live there for couple of years, before expected opening of the London office of 'House of Al-Zor'. He had no idea that only a short distance away, almost at the same time; Meina was also going to New York.

'One day you will feel the pain and sorrow,
No one to help you, just your own shadow,
'Tant pis' the time wouldn't stop for you,
Find no one cares, the life is just a shallow. ©

End

Other work By Kamal M Malak

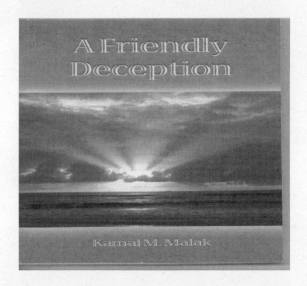